MW01716484

JAZZ'S SONG

OLIVIA RENEE WALLACE

ISBN: 0985211989
ISBN-13: 978-0-9852119-8-1

DEDICATION

This is dedicated to anyone in search of their own song…

ACKNOWLEDGMENTS

FIVE!

I am now officially five novels deep! This is still an amazing journey for me. I am so blessed to be able to continue doing what I love in this industry! Though I still consider myself as a small fish in this big pond, I am growing and I want to send a quick thank you to those who have helped me along the way.

Of course, thanks will always go to my "Home Team": my mom (Jean) and my girls (Devon, Dasia, and Ajanni), who all had to put up with me as I put in the work to finish this book. I love you all and thank you for your patience. Thank you to my sis, Dez, for always telling her friends about my work.

And of course, a HUGE shout out to my honey Sean who brought my cover to life again and Carla Dean, my editor who came through and got it done for me when I needed it! I couldn't have finished this without you!

My betas: Andrea, Aija, Chandra, and ADRIENNE (your input was priceless). I appreciate you all for always giving me constructive criticism and motivation. You ladies are awesome!

Anjella, thank you for ALWAYS being so supportive and enthusiastic about my work. Samantha Flemons, thank you for your support and always sharing my work! Ebony Evans and the ladies of EYECU, thank you for keeping me motivated and keeping my creative mojo flowing (Freestyle Fridays rock!) Ebonee Abby, thank you for looking out for a chick. I swear we are gonna do lunch one day! And Mrs. Joyce Dickerson, thank you for looking out for me from my first book event until now. I appreciate you all! There are many others I'd love to name, but if I keep going, you'll never get to read the book! I appreciate you all greatly!

ISSUES

I can't say love has always been a friend of mine. It would probably be more accurate to say I didn't really know what love was, although I thought I did. I'm assuming I was wrong, though. Or maybe love didn't know me. I'd dealt with different kinds of relationships: romantic, friendships, family. But, it seemed like I received the short end of the stick when it came to basking in that fuzzy feeling folks refer to as "love". It was like waiting at the end of a long line, and by the time it was my turn to receive it, only scraps were left. Just enough for me to sample but not really enjoy.

In my life, I can only recall two people who actually loved me. I mean the *real* deal. They were my mother and my grandmother. Even then, I was cheated because they were both taken from me way too soon.

When I was seven, my father shot my mother because she wanted to leave him. After years of his beatings followed with "Please forgive me" gifts and "It'll never happen again" promises, she couldn't take it anymore. She planned to take me and flee, but he wasn't having it. After realizing what he had done, he shot himself in the head. I witnessed it all from the crack in the kitchen pantry door. I spent years wondering if I would still be alive if he had known I was watching. I spent even more years weighed down by guilt because I wasn't able to save her.

After the tragic death of my mother, my grandmother took me in. For two years, I ate three meals a day, attended church every Sunday and afterwards helped set the table for dinner, and learned as many bible stories and lessons on life as my young mind could handle. She helped fill the void that was left when my mother died. No, nothing can replace a mother's love, but it was love nonetheless. I felt safe with my grandmother, and I needed that. For two years, she provided the love and protection that I needed to survive. Then…she was gone.

Her health quickly declined. She had diabetes, high blood pressure, and who knows how many other ailments. It happened so fast. She went from feeling tired and dizzy, to laying in a hospital bed, to never stepping foot out of the hospital. She was the last person that I'd known to ever truly love me.

After that, I was shifted around from family member to family member. They attempted to keep me out of the system, but there was always a breaking point. Being a little "different", I was just too much for them. Either they had their own kids to worry about, or they didn't know how to handle me considering all that I had already been through. At least, those were the reasons they verbally expressed. There was always *something*, though. Not to say they didn't care. They just hadn't cared *enough.*

It was only a matter of time before I ended up in foster care. After bouncing from home to home, it finally dawned on me that most of the foster parents didn't care either. They only took me in for the benefits. By the time I turned sixteen, I made it my business to make them work for those benefits, though. I got in with a bad crowd, thinking of myself as a little gangster, and had a couple of run-ins with the law that resulted in me finding myself in juvie on more than one occasion.

Then there came Ms. Tracy Smith, a caseworker who took me under her wing. She told me that she didn't want me to be the stereotype.

"*You have too much potential*," she had told me more than once.

"*How do you know?*" I always asked her.

"*Because I know,*" she would respond.

Believing her, I straightened up my act. She helped me get into a program, and I got my GED. I started to believe there was someone on Earth who cared about me again. So, when she transferred out of her department and moved to another county, it felt like the ultimate act of betrayal.

For a year, I held on to my animosity, but I let it go when I finally saw her again. By that time, she was no longer Ms. Smith. She'd gotten married and became Mrs. Cross. Hence the reason she moved away. Hell, I hadn't even known she was in a relationship. It stung a little when she told me that she keeps her personal life separate from her work. I guess it was silly of me to think I had been more to her than just a case. Still, I tried to make myself understand things from her perspective.

Using some of her old connections, she helped me once again and advised me to get myself together *for good.* I promised her that I would.

With her help, I got a small apartment and found a job that helped me get by. She told me the rest would be up to me and that she would keep in contact. That was almost ten years ago.

True to her word, she kept in contact. She called every few

months to check up on me and let me know how she was doing. Though we stayed in touch, we hadn't seen each other in person since the day she co-signed on my first lease.

About halfway through this ten-year time span, *she* came into my life. *Jordan Davis.*

She's the reason I decided there was one thing I would never do again after her, and that's give my heart to another girl.

Jordan was fine as hell, thick in all the right places. Her face was flawless, makeup always on point. Full, glossy lips. She dressed in what was the latest fashions and always kept her hair nicely done. I thought she was a young Aphrodite.

And Aphrodite had noticed *me.*

I was still coming into myself and dealing with the fact that I wasn't just a tomboy. I was a woman who preferred girls. I had played around a little but never gone all the way with a woman. A few kisses here and there, maybe a little bit of touching, but that had been about it. I enjoyed it so much, though! My only other "intimate" experience had been with a guy, which went horribly wrong. After that, I refused to let another man lay a finger on me.

It was my freshman year in college. I was slightly older than most of the other freshmen because of having such a late start, but I was still a little naïve about life. She was eighteen, and I was twenty-one. We had a class together, and she'd sat near me.

For the first week or so, I noticed she kept looking at me. At first, I was flattered. That is until she finally spoke to me. She caught me coming out of the small auditorium.

"Excuse me," she said, touching my arm to stop me just as I was about to walk past her.

She smiled and my stomach flipped.

"Your name is Jasmine, right?"

"Yeah," I answered, surprised she even knew my name.

"I'm Jordan," she said, extending her hand.

I accepted it and shook it briefly. It was so warm and soft.

"Can I help you with something?" I asked, certain she hadn't stopped me just to confirm my name.

"Kinda," she replied somewhat hesitantly. "Actually, it's something that could help both of us."

"Oh?" Having no idea what she was talking about, I waited for her to continue.

"Well," she began, clearing her throat, "I noticed you have a shitload of hair, and you always have it pulled back in this huge ponytail," she said, pointing at my head. "I wanted to extend my services to you."

"Your services?" I asked, momentarily lost.

"Yeah," she said with a nod. "I do hair. It's my side hustle to make a little extra change. I thought maybe you could use my services."

"Oh," I responded in a flat tone.

Self-consciously, my hand automatically went to my hair. I had inherited a blend of my mother and father's hair. I got her thickness, and the waves came from his biracial heritage. I also managed to get his light complexion in spite of my mother being beautifully brown-skinned. My wavy hair had always been an issue for me, and even at the age of twenty-two, I hadn't mastered taming it. So, I always threw it into a ponytail and kept it moving.

"I'm sorry," she said quickly, pulling me out of my thoughts. "I didn't mean to offend you."

"You didn't," I told her, not quite able to make eye contact. Here I was thinking about how fine she was, and she was thinking how I looked a hot mess.

"I don't believe you, but okay," she replied. "Well, let me make up for it. Let me braid it for you. I won't even charge you the first time."

"So that's supposed to make me feel better?" I asked with a slight laugh.

It had been ages since anyone had touched my hair, but if I must be honest, if she braided it, it would mean I wouldn't have to worry about it for at least a week. Hell, I was completely down for that.

"I guess that would be cool," I told her, trying to sound nonchalant.

"That's what's up," she told me and smiled again.

We exchanged numbers and met up at my apartment that night after I got off from work. As she braided my hair, we had a pleasant conversation, and I warmed up to her really quick.

I started getting my hair braided every other week after that. It made life a little easier for me, but that wasn't my only reason. I got it done to be around her. It felt good having someone to talk to who wasn't just some cat in the hood. She was a college girl, and we had good conversations about everything from school to music, movies, and current affairs. She stretched my brain, and I loved it.

We started spending time together outside of her doing my hair. She lived in the dorms but came over to my apartment off campus as often as possible. She'd told me that she really liked being around me, and I told her that I felt the same.

She started telling me that I was one of her closest friends, and of course, I started falling in love. I eventually gave her a key to my place, and she started doing her clients' heads there.

That's how I met JB Donovan, who would end up becoming my best friend. Jordan kept JB's dreadlocks fresh. JB was what most folks considered a dom, and she was proud of it. She was one of the coolest cats that I had met in my life. She was something of a chick magnet with her cocoa-colored skin, long locs, and confident personality. She started to rub off on me in a positive way.

And she tried to warn me about Jordan.

"Be careful with that one," she told me one night while we were playing video games at my apartment.

"What are you talking about?" I asked her as I tried to keep my focus on Grand Theft Auto.

"You're into her," she answered. "It's written all over your face."

"Is that a bad thing?" I wanted to know.

"It is if you don't really know what you're dealing with," she replied, then paused the game and looked at me. "Look, lil' baby stud—"

"Why I gotta be all that?" I interrupted with a laugh. "I'm older than you."

"Yeah, but you're still new to this," she threw back at me. "Like I was saying, I went to school with her, and we grew up in the same neighborhood. She's cool, but I've never seen her be with anyone for more than a month or two. She gets around. I'm not saying she's fucking everybody, but she loses interest real quick. And you know she goes both ways, right?"

"What's that gotta do with anything?"

"Nothing," she answered. "If it doesn't bother you, then cool. I just try to keep away from them flippity-floppety chicks, but that's my choice. But anyway! You're clearly in love with Jordan, and she's not the fall-in-love type from what I've seen. So, just be careful. Don't say I didn't warn you."

"I hear ya," I told her, returning my attention to my game.

I heard her, but I didn't listen. For a while, I was glad I hadn't.

Eventually, I told Jordan how I felt. We were in my living room eating pizza and watching a show on television before she got started on my hair. A commercial had come on. That's when I decided to test the water a bit.

"Hey, Jordan," I began, "I've never asked, but are you seeing someone?"

She laughed. "No. When would I have time? I'm almost always over here."

"Well, is there anybody who you might be interested in?"

"Why do you ask?" she wanted to know.

Since I had already put my toe in the water, I went ahead and dove in.

"I've been trying to play it cool, but I'm really feeling you, Jordan," I confessed. "I hope this doesn't mess up our friendship, but I couldn't keep holding it in."

I watched a smile slowly form on her lips.

"Really?" she asked.

"Yeah, really."

"Well," she began, "if you must know, I'm feeling you, too."

"Really?" I responded with surprise.

"Really," she answered, still smiling.

"So now what?" I asked.

"How about we start with a kiss?"

I had butterflies in my stomach as our lips met. It started so simple and gentle, but it quickly grew into something else. I felt a hunger, a yearning I wasn't quite prepared for. She, on the other hand, was better prepared.

She rose from the sofa and held out her hand. When I took it, she led me to my bedroom. My nerves were on high alert; I felt like a complete virgin.

"Um, look, Jordan," I said hesitantly. "This is all still kinda new to me—"

She placed her finger on my lips. "Shhh. I'll guide you along the way."

And she did.

Over time, she taught me how to please her and proved that she knew how to please me, also. We learned each other's bodies and elicited the perfect response out of one another. It never even occurred to me to be concerned that an eighteen-year-old had so much experience. All that mattered to me was she wanted me as much as I wanted her.

We even went shopping together for my first strap. I remember being so nervous the first time I used it, but it quickly became second nature. She loved every stroke I put on her. It was an ego boost for me, and my attitude changed a bit with my growing confidence. Then I started dressing a little different. I retired my customary sweats, and she went with me when I shopped for a new wardrobe. My whole swagger was different.

I was so in love, and I was sure she was in love with me, too. After all, she had stuck around way longer than JB said she would. We were together nearly six months before I confessed that I loved her. We made love afterwards; the act was so deep and passionate that it almost left me breathless.

From there, it was all downhill.

She became distant and barely acknowledged me in class. Suddenly, she was always busy, so we weren't spending nearly as much time together. Text messages became the norm instead of phone calls. Finally, she came to the apartment…to get her things.

"This isn't working," she'd said. "I care about you. I really do. I just think we've done too much too fast."

I saw her the very next day after class. When I tried to talk to her, she seemed to be in a rush to get away from me. I soon found out why. Her ride was waiting for her. I watched her climb into the car, and she had the nerve to look uncomfortable as the guy in the driver's seat leaned over to give her a quick kiss.

I was furious!

I can't recall how many messages and text messages I sent

her, letting her know how much of a treacherous whore I thought she was. I cursed her out. I called her until she had her number changed. I burned the few pics I had of us.

I was so full of anger. I was so full of hurt.

JB tried to console me, but the "I told you so" was written all over her face even though she never said it aloud.

I vowed I would never allow myself to get wrapped up in another woman again, and I meant it.

This love shit was bullshit.

The soundtrack of my life was titled *Fuck Love.*

All love had ever caused me was pain anyway.

MOVING DAY

It had been a long time coming, but it was happening. I was buying my first home. It wasn't much, just a two-bedroom in Jonesboro. But, it had a fenced-in backyard that was big enough for me to have the occasional get-together. Most importantly, it would be all mine.

I would be paying a mortgage on my home and not be paying rent for someone else's. There would be no loud neighbors above me banging around while I was trying to sleep. There would be nobody knocking on the door, asking for sugar or some other trivial shit while I was trying to get a piece of pretty pie. On nights when I wanted to turn up my music, there would be nobody in the next room ready to complain about the music coming through the thin walls.

I would be free.

The paperwork had been completed, and all I had to do was pick up my keys. I couldn't even front like I wasn't overjoyed.

"So when do you want to start moving stuff?"

"ASAP."

I was shooting a game of hoops with JB on a warm Saturday afternoon, and we were taking a break in between games.

"I pick up the keys on Monday," I told my friend. "I've already started boxing shit up. I went to get the utilities handled yesterday, so I'm going to start moving my stuff in Monday morning as soon as I get those keys."

"I know you're excited as hell," she said.

"You already know it! I tried to show you the house, but you be so busy now since you're living the *family life*."

"Don't even act like that," she responded, laughing. "You just caught me on an off day that one time. Don't be all dramatic. Married or not, I still make time for my homie."

"Yeah, yeah," I said with a snort. "So how is my godbaby doing anyway? I haven't seen her in about a month."

"She's supposed to start preschool next month, but Nelle's bullshittin'." JB smirked. "She claims she's cool, but she ain't gonna be able to handle Kay-Kay being at a school all damn day. She was a mess when she first went back to work, and her mother was keeping Kay-Kay then. She's not going to be able to cope with strangers teaching our baby."

Kayla, better known as Kay-Kay, was the daughter of JB and her wife, Shanelle. She was the beautiful product of a relationship that had been hella complicated for a while. But, my friends finally got it together, and they were now the poster children for the "new" modern family. At least they were most of the time. Kayla appealed to my maternal instincts from time to time and made me wish for what I had always thought couldn't be.

I was so emotionally screwed up, it never occurred to me that I could be a good parent to a child. So, she was as close as I thought I would ever get to being remotely maternal. It felt odd sometimes, but I watched her on rare occasions so my friends could have a night out or whatever they chose to do. I'd buy her a happy meal and put the same cartoon on repeat, and she'd be so content that folks would swear I knew what I was doing.

But, really, I was just winging it and doing what JB and Shanelle had told me to do. She was potty-trained and always fell asleep on her own by 7:30 p.m., so she was never a bother. And she smiled at me like she had absolutely no issue with an auntie who looked like a tomboy.

"What about you?" I asked JB. "Are you going to be able to handle her being at school with a bunch of strangers?"

"Oh, I can handle it," she answered. "I don't have a problem at all poppin' up at the preschool, and they better have their shit together."

"I hear ya," I responded with a laugh.

"What?" she wanted to know.

"Who would've thought JB Donovan would end up being Mr. Mom?"

"Right!" she said, laughing herself. "I never would've pictured it either, but I wouldn't trade it for anything. The player shit gets old, ya know."

"No, I don't know," I retaliated. "I'm cool holding on to my player card."

"You say that now," JB debated. "You just haven't come across the right one yet, that's all."

"I ain't lookin' either," I told her. "But, about this move…"

"I got you," she said, shaking her head at me.

"Don't be shaking your head like you weren't running the streets with me."

"I know," she said. "I just knew when to say when."

"Yeah, yeah, yeah," I answered. "You didn't have it all figured out so smoothly. I remember you being with crazy-ass Monique."

She winced. "Ooh! I dodged a bullet with that one, huh?"

"Right," I said with a victorious smile. "I told you there was something about her that wasn't on the up and up. Sometimes I actually know what *I'm* talking about."

"Ten o'clock, Monday morning?" she asked, changing the subject.

"Sounds good," I answered with a knowing smile.

"One more game?" she suggested.

"Let's do it."

Monday couldn't come fast enough. Like a kid on Christmas morning, I was up before my alarm went off. I could hardly wait to get the keys to the big present I had bought for myself.

I sprung out of bed and brushed my teeth. After looking in the mirror, I decided to touch up my Caesar-style cut.

After breaking up with Jordan, the first thing I did was go to the nearest barbershop and cut my hair to start the healing process. She loved my hair so much and always played in it. The last thing I wanted to do was think about those times. I remember wanting to cry while watching my long tresses hit the floor, but the deed had been done. To my surprise, when I looked in the mirror afterwards and took in the low cut, I fell in love with it. I've been wearing it low with no regrets ever since.

I loved it so much that after getting my bachelor's degree in psychology, I went to barbering school and got my license to cut hair. I found it ironic that what my ex had done for a side hustle, and what brought us together in the first place, had become my passion. And I was damn good at what I did. I've even won a competition or two.

After making sure my cut was satisfactory, I jumped in the

shower to cleanse my body and wash the excess hair off my skin. Once dressed, I put my few toiletries in a small duffle bag. Then, I cleaned the bathroom, took down the shower curtain, and removed the rugs, putting them in a separate bag. The bathroom was cleaner than when I had moved in.

Hungry, I ate a bowl of cereal and had a glass of juice. Then, I washed the few dishes that were in the sink and boxed them up. After sealing up the box with packing tape, I placed it near the front door until I was ready to take it outside and put it in the backseat of my car with some of the other small boxes I already had packed up.

By the time nine o'clock came around, I had my car filled to capacity and was sitting at my realtor's office waiting for her to arrive.

My heartbeat quickened as she pulled up next to me less than a minute later. She stepped out of her car, and I did the same.

She looked at her watch and laughed. "Excited, are we?"

"Is it that obvious?" I asked, following her as she started walking towards the entrance.

As she unlocked the door to the building, she looked over her shoulder, smiled at me, and replied, "It's just a guess." She opened the glass door and flipped a switch as we entered the building. "I apologize for running a little late. Nellie usually has everything up and running by now, but I gave her the day off."

"It's no problem," I told her. "I had just pulled up right before you did. I'm just excited about getting the keys to my first spot."

"And you should be!" she said, going into her office and turning the light on. "This is a big deal! You're not even thirty yet, and you've acquired your first home. There are people who are twice your age who are still trying to do that. It's pretty impressive, really."

"Thank you." I felt my face get warm at the compliment.

The more I thought about it, it really was a big accomplishment considering where I had been only ten years prior. From foster child to delinquent. From a young woman on the verge of breaking down to becoming a student. From a student to a college graduate to becoming a Master Barber. And now, I was a homeowner. For a second, I was in awe of myself.

She sat down behind her desk, and I took a seat in front of it. After going over a few things, she held out the keys to me. My hands shook a little as I accepted them.

"If there's anything else I can assist you with, don't hesitate to call me, okay?" she told me. "You have my cell."

"Can I give you a hug?" I asked her, slightly nervous.

"I think that would be appropriate for this occasion," she responded with a chuckle before coming from behind her desk.

I stood up and gave her the biggest hug I could without hurting her, of course. "Thank you so much for everything, Joi."

"It has been my pleasure," she said, hugging me almost like a mother would. "A friend of Nellie and JB is a friend of mine. I mean it. If there's anything I can help you with, don't hesitate to ask."

"Okay," I told her with a nod. "Thank you again."

"You're so welcome," she replied. "Enjoy your new home."

My hand trembled slightly as I inserted the key in the keyhole. I'm not sure if nervousness or excitement had my stomach doing flips as I turned the key. I had been there before, more than once actually. But, it felt different this time. Now the house was mine.

Maybe I was nervous because of the new responsibilities I would be taking on. If something went wrong, I would have to figure it out for myself since there would be no landlord for me to call. At the same time, I wouldn't be handing over rent money to a landlord. My mortgage was actually less than the rent I had been paying for my last apartment. So, I would be saving money. Hell, I could probably afford to go on a decent vacation with the money I would be saving.

I looked around and took in the updates Joi McIntosh had put into my home. When I first saw it, I noticed it needed a little work, but something about the house called to me. So, when she told me that she could help me lock down this house, I was all for it. My realtor also had experience in home design and decoration, and she promised I would love what she did with it.

She had kept her word. The like-new stove and side-by-side refrigerator, updated fireplace, resurfaced countertops, freshly painted walls, new tiles in both bathrooms, and hardwood floors throughout the rest of the house made me feel like I had been chosen for one of those home renovation shows. A tinge of paint could still be smelled in the air along with a fruity scent that wafted from an air freshener plugged into an outlet near where I had already planned to put my microwave.

I did a little dance while checking out each room in *my* house. I looked out of the wood and glass patio door that led to *my* backyard and took a deep breath, feeling like I was on top of the world.

I'm really in my own place.

Remembering that I had to meet JB back at my apartment, I ran out to my car and started unloading it. I quickly put the boxes inside along with several bags that held most of my clothes. Then I hurried and locked the door so I wouldn't keep JB waiting. JB had a truck, so I ended up not having to rent one, and with her willing to work for pizza and beer, the set-up was perfect.

I was walking to my car, when I heard her speak to me.

"Hi, new neighbor!"

I looked up and almost had to pause. Something about her made my breath catch in my throat.

She wasn't what I was accustomed to by physical standards. My type were chicks who bordered on being dimes, the model-looking type. She wasn't that, at least not by traditional standards. However, she was pretty nonetheless. She was a little on the thicker side; I would guess maybe a size sixteen or so. From where I stood, her brown skin beamed in the sunlight, and her friendly smile outshined it.

I smiled and waved back. *She might possibly be a perk for moving into the neighborhood.*

That thought was short-lived as I watched a man come out of her front door and give her a kiss before making his way to get in his car. He glanced my way and quickly dismissed me as he revved up his engine.

I climbed in my car and started it up. *Oh well*, I thought to myself. *It's probably better this way, Jazz. You shouldn't play where you stay.*

It could've turned into an issue if we had messed around and she got all in her feelings. I wasn't looking for anything serious; I just wanted to have a nice time with some feminine company.

I shook my head at my own presumptuousness. Just

because she gave me a friendly hello, it didn't mean she wanted me to play in her cat. Sometimes I was too cocky for my own good. I laughed and humbled myself.

It would be nice to have a neighbor who spoke whenever they saw me in my yard or had a cup of sugar I could borrow, if needed. In that moment, she seemed like she might be a nice neighbor, so I would let her be just that. Besides, who said she wanted to be more than that anyway? She could've been as straight as a board…or maybe a total *spaghetti chick*. Straight until hot and wet.

I laughed at my thoughts while driving to my apartment. I hadn't even said a word to her and was already drumming up scenarios.

I think I'm overdue for getting laid.

I added it to my to-do list as I pulled into a parking space in front of my apartment, soon to be my old place of residence. There were a number of women that I could call who knew how to deal with me. They knew what to expect from me and vice versa. Once I got settled into my new spot, I would utilize one of those numbers.

Returning my focus to the task at hand, I climbed out of my car and found JB already backed in and sitting on the back of the truck, waiting for me.

"How long have you been here?" I asked as I walked up to her.

"Just a few minutes," she answered, not looking up. She was focused on some game on her phone. "You ready?" she asked, her eyes still glued to the screen.

"Whenever you are," I told her. "I see you're completely enthralled in your mobile device, so I'll be in the apartment grabbing some more stuff to put in my car."

"I'm coming," she said. "I'm almost done."

"Yeah, yeah, yeah," I replied, then made my way into the breezeway to unlock my front door. I had just picked up a box containing my movies and games, when she came into the apartment. "I'm glad you could join me," I said with sarcasm as I hoisted the box up higher for a better grip.

She laughed. "I told you I was coming. You need help with that?"

"I got this," I told her. "You can grab those pictures that are leaning against the wall over there though, if you wanna."

She looked around and whistled. "You weren't playing when you said you were already getting stuff together."

"Hell naw," I told her. "I'm ready to get the hell outta here."

JB laughed as she made her way over to the group of framed pictures near my sofa. She followed me out and slid the frames into the trunk that I had popped open with my key fob.

"What else is going in the trunk?" she wanted to know.

"The clothes I've got hanging in the closet," I answered. "I'll grab them. Then, we can go ahead and move the big shit."

"Well, let's do the damn thang!"

"Let's do the damn thang then!"

It took three trips and a little over two hours to move the furniture from my bedroom, living room, and dining room, but we got it all moved. I was so glad I had lived on the first floor of that apartment building.

While we were putting my bed together, the doorbell rang. I went to the door and found Shanelle and Kayla standing there. She held a pizza and a plastic bag, and Kayla had her little arms wrapped around a two-liter bottle of root beer.

"Hey!" I said, unlocking the screen door and opening it

for them. "Hey, JB," I yelled. "We've got food! Special delivery!"

"Hey, baby," she said, coming out of my room to greet her wife. She gave her a kiss before picking up their daughter for a hug.

"Ma, you smell funny," Kayla told her.

"That's what hard work smells like," JB said before placing her back on the floor.

The little scene was cute. Not exactly my type of party, but it was cute regardless.

"You got a hug for me?" I asked my goddaughter.

"Auntie Jazz!" she shouted gleefully before running to me for a hug.

I can't even lie. It made me feel good.

After giving me a hug, she said, "You smell funny, too."

"It's my new cologne," I told her. "It's called *Le Sweat*. You don't like it?"

"Nuh-uh!" she said, grimacing. "You should get some perfume like Mama. She always smells good."

"I'll try to remember that," I said as solemnly as I could. "I promise to smell better the next time you see me. Okay?"

"Okay," she said with a smile, satisfied that she had given me some good advice. Then, she turned to Shanelle and asked, "Can we eat now?"

"Yes, ma'am," Shanelle answered.

"I have to go find my dishes," I told her, about to head toward the kitchen.

"No, you don't," she said, stopping me. "We got napkins, paper plates, and plastic cups. So, we got you covered. Y'all go wash your hands so we can eat while the pizza is still hot."

"My baby thinks of everything," JB stated proudly. "I keep telling you, you ought to get one of your own!"

"Yeah, I hear ya," I said, brushing off her comment as we went to wash our hands.

I watched them as we ate lunch and drank sodas. They looked so happy.

JB had been a certified player when we were in college. We both had experienced heartbreaks, and after that, we vowed not to get so wrapped up in women. But, Shanelle quickly changed that. My friend fell and fell hard for the chick who had been in the closet. They had split up for a little while and gotten into new relationships. Shanelle's resulted in Kayla's birth, and even after that, they managed to find their way back to each other. It had been a modern fairytale and most certainly a beautiful thing.

But, shit like that didn't happen to people like me.

The love they had for each other was so surreal that it never occurred to me that I could attain it. It was like their whole relationship was the product of one of those romance novels.

Hell, it had been so long since I had experienced any type of family life that I wasn't even sure I knew how to be a family member much less someone's rock, love, or protector.

I wasn't cut out for that whole family thing. Or so I thought.

Little did I know I was about to be put to the test.

A FEW MINUTES

It's amazing how life can change so quickly. I mean, it can literally change in a matter of minutes.

Sometimes a person can have their whole life planned out from the time they're in school until when they plan to retire. Somebody else's plan may be having no real plan at all, playing it by ear and seeing what happens. Then there are those select few who don't care one way or another.

I was somewhere between the latter two.

At least I was when I was between sixteen and seventeen years old.

Being in and out of the system had done something to my soul. A tiny part of me always wanted to hope that good things would come my way, while another part of me just didn't give a damn. But, life had plans in store for me that I had not prepared for.

The stints in juvenile hall should have been enough for me, but I had to learn the hard way about life. I had to learn to be more concerned about the company that I kept.

There was this guy who they called Rich. I never knew if it was a nickname or his real name, but he hung out with the crew that I called myself running with. He was in his twenties and always kept a big knot of money on him. In spite of me then having my tomboyish demeanor, he took an interest in me.

Young and dumb, I started looking up to him as something like a brother figure. After all, he had given me money, bought me food, purchased me some shoes and a jacket, and even made sure I had all the weed and liquor my naïve little heart desired. It seemed like he cared for me more than any of my foster parents had.

By the time I realized I was being bought myself, it was too late.

He had gotten a motel room for me and the rest of the clique, and we'd all been smoking, drinking, and partying it up. Everybody got pretty fucked up, and most of them had passed out. Rich and I were the last two standing.

I remember trying to get comfortable in the chair that I had been sitting in. I had my feet propped up on the queen-sized bed that two of the other kids were knocked out on. Rich was sitting in the other chair opposite me.

"You don't look comfortable," he'd said.

"I'm good," I told him, still trying to adjust myself in the seat.

"Naw. No, you ain't," he said, then stood up. "Come with me. I got another room. It's got two beds, too. One for you and one for me. I know you don't wanna be cramped up in that chair and stuck in here with these musty fools."

"Word?" I replied, never even considering I was about to walk into the lion's den. Hell, I was excited about being in another room without the clutter of my other associates.

I jumped up from the chair, grabbed my small bag of belongings, and followed Rich, actually feeling grateful for the concern of my "play brother".

I followed him down the walkway to another room. He pulled out his key and opened the door. True to his word, there were two queen-sized beds in the room. The room was nice and clean compared to the one we had just left, and all I could think about was taking a nice, hot shower.

"This is straight," I told him, nodding my head in approval.

I dropped my bag on the bed that I was claiming and grabbed the remote to the television. After finding a movie, I kicked back on the bed while Rich sat at the small table and filled a blunt with some mid-grade marijuana.

"You gonna hit this?" he asked after lighting it up and taking a drag.

"Duh," I told him before hopping off my bed and sitting on the side of his.

We passed the blunt back and forth a few times before I'd had enough.

"I'm straight. I'm gonna go hop in the shower."

"That's what's up," he said, standing up. "I'ma go catch these vending machines while you in the shower. You want something?"

"Hell, yeah!" I answered enthusiastically.

"Well, what you want?" he asked.

I paused and rubbed my chin as if in deep thought before answering. "Er'rythang!"

We both laughed.

"You stupid," he said, while walking towards the door. "I'll be back."

"Alright then," I said, then grabbed my bag and headed to the bathroom for a long, hot shower. When I came out twenty minutes later, I felt high, hungry, and clean.

Rich was laying on his bed with his eyes closed, so I figured he was knocked out. I found chips, cookies, candy bars, and sodas on the table. I killed most of it before laying on my bed and nodding off myself.

At first, I thought I was dreaming when I felt my sweats being tugged down my legs, but it became a real nightmare really quick. I tried to sit up.

"Hey, what the fuck—"

"Shhh," he said, pushing me back down.

"Rich, man, I ain't with this," I told him.

My nerves were instantly on red alert. My stomach started churning when I tried once more to sit up and he pushed me back down.

"Hush," he said, holding me down by my shoulder. "You got something I want. And I've got something you need."

I strained against his hand, surprised at how strong he was. I was in a daze as he positioned himself on top of me, pinning my legs with his body. When I tried to push at him, he held down both of my hands above my head using just one of his massive hands.

In shock over what was happening, I closed my eyes tightly. I could smell and feel his hot breath on my face as he moved in closer to me.

"Why you wanna act like a nigga?" he demanded. "You so gotdamn pretty. Why you wanna act like a dude?"

I turned my head and kept my mouth and eyes shut tight.

"If you was my girl, I'd take care of you," he kept on.

He kissed me on my neck and growled.

I wanted to throw up.

"Don't do this," I begged as his free hand found the flesh that had been hidden beneath my panties. "Please."

"This is what you need," he said, his fingers digging into the place no one had ever been before. "You just need a nigga to take care of you. I'm that nigga. I've been taking care of you all this time, right? You owe me now. All I want is a few minutes."

I was terrified. I could hardly breathe. My heart was racing. It felt like the room was spinning. I had never felt so helpless.

Then there was nothing.

Nothing but the ache.

I looked to the left, and there he was lying next to me, knocked out with his arm draped over me like it was the most natural thing in the world for him. His arm felt heavy as a log as I eased from under it.

I wobbled a little as I made my way to the bathroom, closing and locking the door behind me. I sat on the toilet and felt the immediate burn when I tried to empty my bladder. My flesh had been torn. I had been violated in the most heinous of ways. I had been robbed of my innocence, the only thing I had left.

Grabbing the wash rag I had hung over the edge of the tub, I turned on the tub's faucet and ran the water as low as possible to keep quiet. Gently, I wiped away the mixture of his bodily fluids and my blood, while silently crying my eyes out. Then, I threw up. Then, I cried some more.

After several attempts to regain my composure, I tip-toed out of the bathroom. Keeping my eyes on his sleeping figure, I quickly put back on the clothes he had so inconsiderately taken off of me. I stepped into the Nike shoes he had paid for and donned the jacket he had also bought.

As I crept to the door, I paused. I turned back around, and for a moment, I could only look at him in disgust. I wanted to grab something and bash his head in, but I was afraid to get that close to him for fear he would wake up. I had already learned he was way stronger than me and I was no competition for him.

I did, however, grab his pants that were balled up on the floor. I reached into one pocket and took the wad of money he'd had on him. I reached into the other pocket, pulled out the bag of weed, and stuffed it into my own pocket. I even snatched his lighter and the remaining bit of snacks from the table, stuffing them into my bag.

As I made my way to the door, I heard him shift in the bed. Hurrying, I left out the door and hobbled away as fast as my battered body would allow me.

That was a memory I always kept tucked away, but it came pushing back into the forefront of my mind as I drove along I-75 south heading to Warner Robins, Georgia.

That's where I found Mrs. Cross months after my incident

with Rich. I felt like she was the only person who I could tell about it. After I left that motel room, I went back to my foster home, and though my foster mom had let me back in after being gone for over a week again, I didn't feel welcomed at all. I left for good after sleeping there for one night. I wasn't close to any of the other kids who lived in that house, so I had nobody to confide in. I was too afraid to go to the cops because Rich had mentioned having a relative on the force, so it was too much of a risk.

Mrs. Cross was the only hope I had.

After skipping around from place to place for months, I finally found her. Her husband was in the Air Force, and they had a home in the military town of Warner Robins. She was surprised when she found me at her front door.

"I didn't know where else to go," I said as a greeting while she stared at me in shock.

I was so afraid she would turn me away, but she didn't. Instead, she stepped to the side and told me to come in. She and her husband took care of me for nearly three months, and she helped me get on my feet. I knew I would owe her forever.

As I drove to her home for the first time in ten years, I knew it was time to pay the piper.

I thought about the phone call from her as I entered the city limits.

"Jasmine," she had said. "I need to see you. It's time."

I wanted to object, but I already owed her so much. Even though I hadn't made any plans as far as going to see her, I knew she would eventually call and I couldn't stay away forever.

I just hadn't been prepared for what she would say.

My stomach churned as I walked up the steps to the house

where I lived for a couple of months a decade ago. My hand trembled as I pressed the doorbell. I wanted to run back to my car and drive away, but I knew I couldn't. I could hear my heartbeat in my ears as I waited for her to answer the door.

I hadn't realized I had been holding my breath until I released it when she opened the door.

"Hello, Jasmine."

She looked almost regal as she stood in the doorway.

"Mrs. Cross."

It was all I could muster at the moment.

She stepped to the side. "Come in."

I followed her into the living room. It still looked the same other than the addition of a few portraits on the walls. Her house still smelled like apples and cinnamon, and for a moment, I let the scent comfort me. I remember how safe she and her husband, Robert, had made me feel during my brief stay. They had been the closest I could remember to having parents in the traditional sense. In that moment, I felt a huge surge of gratitude.

As she took a seat on her sofa, I sat on the nearby loveseat.

"How have you been, Jasmine?" she asked, observing me as she waited for my answer.

"I'm doing good," I said quickly. I was nervous as hell, but I continued. "I've been working at the barbershop for almost four years, and I just got my first place. Paid off my car…"

She chuckled. "Calm down," she said with a knowing smile. "This isn't an interview. Relax. Would you like something to drink? I made some iced tea."

Her iced tea had always been the bomb. I went through withdrawals after I had left her home.

"Yes, please."

She rose from her seat. "I'll be right back with it," she told me. "Relax, Jasmine."

A minute or two later, she returned with two glasses of her sweet tea and handed one to me. I took a sip and savored the taste before speaking.

"How's Mr. Cross?"

"He's great," she answered. "He should be here any minute now. He's one of the reasons why I asked you to come."

"Oh?" I said.

"Yes," she responded. "We are shipping out of here," she explained. "We will be leaving in two months, heading to California. We're putting the house up for sale, and we plan to make California our permanent home."

"Oh."

"We knew this time would eventually come," she continued. "I've thought long and hard about it. But, I think it is time for you to step up to the plate. I think you are more than ready now."

We heard the front door open and the keys jingling as they were removed from the lock.

"Well, there they are now," she said, rising from her seat. "Are you ready?"

"For what?" I asked.

Even though I already knew the answer, I needed some kind of confirmation.

"To meet Lyric," she answered. "Your daughter."

LYRIC

I couldn't breathe. I struggled to push the air from my lungs to my throat and out of my mouth or nose, but my body wasn't cooperating. I watched as Mr. Cross and the pretty girl came into view.

The girl was chattering away, telling Mr. Cross about her day at gymnastics. She draped her pink duffle bag over her left shoulder and bounced around as she proudly told how she nailed a short routine she'd been working on.

She was so excited and animated.

And beautiful.

I was in awe. She was me, but not.

She was almost the spitting image of me when I was her age. However, her complexion was a little darker than mine. She got that from the predator whose seed invaded my womb. But, everything else was mine. The dimple in her left cheek matched my own. Her thick hair was almost the exact same texture as mine, but her waves were tamed, styled in two perfect French braids that fell past her shoulders. I could see the sparkle in her brown eyes in spite of the distance between us.

Also, she was softer. You could tell by the light in her eyes that she had no worries. She knew what love felt like. She looked happy, vibrant, and full of life.

"Hey, loves," Mrs. Cross spoke to them. "We have company."

They all turned and looked in my direction.

"Jasmine!" Mr. Cross greeted me jubilantly. He walked over and gave me a brief but firm hug. "Long time, no see!"

"Yes, sir. It's been a while," I replied, finally able to release my breath. "How have you been, Mr. Cross?"

"Now, I told you a long time ago to call me Rob," he said back. "That hasn't changed. But, I'm doing good. And you?"

"I'm doing pretty good," I answered. "I won't complain."

"Lyric," Mrs. Cross began, "are you going to speak, baby?"

The girl looked at me curiously for a moment, then raised her hand shyly.

"Hi," she said quietly.

"Hi," I said just as quietly, waving back.

She then looked at Mrs. Cross. "Can I go to my room now, Nana?"

"Yeah, go ahead, baby," Mrs. Cross answered. "And get washed up. Dinner will be ready in a few minutes."

"Yes, ma'am." She glanced at me one more time before moving along.

I stood in silence for a minute before asking, "Nana?"

"Yes," Mrs. Cross replied. "Nana. She knows I'm not her mother, and she knows Robert isn't her father. She's grown up with the knowledge that her mother was away and would come back for her one day. She only knows Rob and me as her grandparents. That's how we raised her."

I sat back down on the loveseat, absorbing the new information.

"Does she know who I am?" I asked.

"I think she might have a clue," she answered. "She has a

picture that she keeps of you, but you looked a little different then."

"A picture?" I questioned, slightly confused. "A picture from where?"

"A picture I took shortly after you had her," Rob answered as he sat down next to his wife. "It was the one and only time I'd seen you hold her."

"I don't remember you taking any pictures," I said, looking at him.

"You wouldn't," he replied. "You didn't know I took it. You were so enchanted by her that you never even noticed."

My mind went back to the time when she was born.

I'd gone into labor almost two months early. I was so afraid for her.

When I first found out I was pregnant, I almost had an abortion, but I got scared at the last minute and didn't go through with it. Even though the night I conceived was the worst experience in my life, something in my heart wouldn't let me abort my baby. Still, I didn't think I would be able to take care of it. I didn't know how to love, and all babies need love. I was young, inexperienced and, in my own mind, a juvenile delinquent.

I was almost five months along when I found Mrs. Cross. I was grateful when she and her husband welcomed me with open arms. Scared, I wanted her help to put the baby up for adoption. I could only hope the baby would have better luck in the system than I did. I'd heard that babies are more likely to be adopted than older kids, so she would have a fighting chance.

With Mrs. Cross' help, I got healthcare, WIC, and she helped me find a place since I had turned eighteen. Her only stipulation was that I stayed with them until the baby was born. I guess she didn't want to chance me doing anything stupid.

When I went into labor early, I was terrified, but the Crosses were there with me all the way. She weighed four pounds and was so tiny that I was afraid to hold her, so I refused. She was in the NICU for several days before I finally got the nerve up to hold her. Once again, they were right there.

As I held her, tears rolled down my face. She was so tiny. So precious.

And I was giving her away.

I couldn't give her what she needed, and I wanted her to have more than what I had.

My eyes were still full of tears when I gave her back to the nurse.

I went into the waiting area to compose myself. It was then that the Crosses offered to take guardianship of Lyric Yvette Richardson. Feeling like a weight had been lifted off of my shoulders, I immediately agreed.

"You don't want to just send her off to some strangers," Mrs. Cross had declared. "She will be well taken care of by us, and when you're ready, we will give custody back to you."

"What if I'm never ready?" I asked, still emotional in spite of my relief.

"I saw how you looked at that little girl," Robert said to me. "One day, you will be ready."

So, we made arrangements. And though we kept in contact, any discussion of her was minimal. No photos were sent, and that was by a mutual agreement. My goal was to focus completely on getting myself together so I could be ready for her when the day came for me to assume my responsibility as a mother.

That time was now. And I still wasn't sure if I was ready.

"What am I supposed to do?" I asked the people who had become my daughter's grandparents. "I mean, I knew this day would eventually come, but I am so not prepared."

"You know what," Robert said. "No parent ever really is. Do you think it was easy for us in the beginning? My only child had gone off to college already when you gave us parental rights for Lyric."

"I had never even had children," Mrs. Cross interjected. "Other than my training and occasionally babysitting for family, I was new to being a parent. I was afraid, but if she couldn't be with you, I couldn't see her being anywhere else but with us."

"We had to learn as we went along," Robert continued. "We didn't always get it right, but we've done our best by her. I have a feeling you will do your best, too."

"All I've ever done is watch my goddaughter a couple of times," I said, still trying to get a grip on what was now inevitable.

"Is she still alive?" Robert asked.

"Yeah."

"Well, you must've done something right!"

I had to laugh at that. I then took a deep breath to try to steady my nerves.

"I'm scared," I admitted quietly. "I'm scared as hell. I don't know what to do."

"Why don't you start with introducing yourself to her," Mrs. Cross suggested gently. "She's a very bright young girl, and we've always been open and honest with her. And just like you, she knew this day would eventually come. She has questions that only you can answer. You can handle this. Both of you can."

I sat there on the loveseat and attempted to absorb everything that had been said in the short time I had been there. After being away for ten years, I was about to introduce myself to my daughter.

How would she react? Would she be angry? Did she hate me?

I was afraid to find out, but I knew I had to make a move

of some sort. It was time for me to be an adult about it.

"Can you call her in here?" I asked softly.

"You can go to her," Mrs. Cross replied. "Her room is the one that you used to sleep in. She might be a little more comfortable in her space. You remember where it is?"

"I think so," I answered before standing up.

I felt like I was walking the Green Mile as I proceeded down the hallway to the room that had once been a guestroom for me. The door was cracked, so I peeked in and took in the room for a moment. Gone were the neutral tones from when I slept there. It was drenched in pinks and pastels with posters of girly cartoon characters on the walls. It was a room fit for a young princess.

What the hell am I going to do with a little princess?

True, I'm a woman, and I've never pretended to be anything else, but I had adapted to more masculine things over the years. Hell, I didn't even wear regular panties. I started wearing boxer briefs as soon as I learned how comfortable they were.

How am I going to teach her how to act like a young lady when I'm not sure how to be one myself?

There was so much I was going to have to figure out. It was almost overwhelming, and I had yet to even talk to her.

I could hear my heartbeat in my ears as I raised my hand to gently knock on her door.

"Come in."

I slowly opened the door and stepped inside. I left the door open and stood near it. I didn't want to invade her space too much too soon.

She stared at me for a minute before speaking. "Hi."

"Hello again," I replied. "I'm Jazz."

"I'm Lyric," she replied back.

For a moment, there was an awkward silence. I wasn't sure of what to say.

I watched her walk over to her dresser and go into a box. Then she walked over to me and held out the item she had retrieved.

It was the picture.

"Is this you?" she asked.

My hand was unsteady as I accepted the picture. I stared at it for a minute, the memories flooding back into my mind again. So did the emotions. It felt like a knot had grown in my throat, and I struggled to clear it before answering.

"Yeah," I answered hoarsely. "That's me."

"I thought so," she said matter-of-factly. "When I first looked at you, I thought you were a boy, but then I noticed…"

She cupped her hands in front of her non-existent breasts.

I chuckled. "I'm definitely not a boy. I just look like one sometimes."

"But you are my mom, huh?"

It was more of a statement than a question.

"Yeah, I am."

"Should I call you Mom now?" she wanted to know.

"You don't have to," I told her. "If you're more comfortable calling me Jazz, I'm cool with that. This is kinda new for both of us."

"I was starting to wonder if you would ever come," she stated calmly as she went and sat on her full-sized bed.

I was surprised by her bluntness, but I also appreciated it.

"You can come and sit next to me if you want to," she offered. "You don't have to just stand there."

"Thank you," I told her.

I joined her, sitting at the end of her bed.

"You don't say a lot," she observed.

"I'm not sure what to say," I told her, being as honest as I could be.

"Are you nervous?" she asked, looking up at me.

"A little bit."

"Why?" she wanted to know.

"Because," I answered, "it's our first time meeting. It seems you already know a little about me, but I don't know if you're angry with me or hate me or what."

"Nana and Poppa taught me that it isn't good to hate," she said. "So, I don't hate you. And you're my mom, so I don't think I could ever hate you. I just don't know you."

"Wow," I told her. "Well, that's a start. You seem like a mature little girl."

"I get that a lot," she replied.

I mentally took back my previous opinion. She only looked like me at that age. We were as different as night and day. She was already light years ahead of where I was at her age. She was so mature for a ten-year-old.

We were both quiet again for a minute before I spoke. "If it's alright with you, I would like for us to get to know each other better."

"Me, too," she replied, and for the first time, she smiled at me.

I felt the first chip of ice melt away.

There was a light knock on the open door. We both looked up and saw Mrs. Cross standing there.

"Dinner is ready. Will you be staying for dinner, Jasmine?"

I looked at Lyric and she nodded.

It was decided.

I stuck around for dinner, and we had pleasant conversation. Afterwards, Lyric showed me some of the ribbons she had won in gymnastic competitions. I made a mental note to be sure to fit gymnastics into my budget for her. I was going to try my best to get this right.

After a little more show-and-tell from Lyric, it was time for me to take that ninety-minute drive back to Jonesboro.

"Will you come back soon?" she asked while walking me to the front door.

"I promise to be back soon," I told her. "We have to see each other to get to know each other better, right?"

"Yes, ma'am," she replied.

It felt strange to be referred to as *ma'am*, but I was willing to adjust to it.

"Oh!" she exclaimed suddenly. "I'll be right back!"

She ran off before I could ask any questions.

"How are you feeling?" Mrs. Cross asked, leaning against the wall.

"It's still a lot to take in," I answered. "But, I think I'm okay."

"Good," she said. "We'll talk in a couple of days to make arrangements. I'd like for you to come here and visit a few times. Then, we will go from there to begin transitioning her to your place by the time school starts in Jonesboro."

"Yes, ma'am," I replied with a nod.

Lyric returned and held out two pictures. "These are for you."

It was the picture from the hospital and her most current school picture.

"Poppa can make me another picture of us, and I thought you might want a school picture to put in your pocketbook."

I was amused at the comment about a pocketbook since I carried a wallet, but I was happy she was so considerate.

"Thank you."

"You're welcome," she said proudly. After a pause, she asked, "Can I have a hug?"

It was such an unexpected request. It made me feel some kind of way, but it was a good feeling.

"Sure," I answered with a slight smile.

She shyly wrapped her arms around me and hugged me tight. I returned the favor.

More ice slipped away.

"I'll see you soon, kid," I told her.

"Okay," she said. "Goodnight, Jazz. Thank you for coming to see me."

She said everything with such simplicity. She had such an unusual balance of maturity and innocence that I was already enthralled by it. Plenty of kids had come into the shop before, boys and girls varying in age from toddlers to teens, but I had never come across one quite like Lyric.

My daughter.

I sat in my car for a minute after telling everyone goodnight. The enormity of it all came crashing down on me as I turned the key in the ignition. I rested my head against the steering wheel and cried harder than I had ever in my life. Then, I laughed.

For the first time ever, I said it out loud.

"I'm a mother!"

I laughed a little harder.

"I'm a mom!"

It was weird to say it out loud, so I said it one more time before pulling off.

"I'm a gotdamn mom!"

PREPPING & PEEKING

I don't remember the drive home.

I was still in shock over what happened. I had finally reunited with my daughter. It was becoming easier to say, at least to myself. After ten years of living like I didn't have a child, it was time to be grown.

I was scared as hell. I didn't want to fuck this up.

That night, I tried to look up books online about raising children. But, I quickly came to the conclusion that she was way too old for those *What to Expect* books. And books by psychologists, especially those without children, just didn't sit well with me. I guessed I was really going to have to play it by ear.

The next morning, I went to the barbershop, as usual. I was there at seven because I had a client who came in at 7:15 a.m. like clockwork. As I checked my equipment, my phone chimed. I looked at the message and smiled.

Good morning, Jazz. Nana gave me ur number. ☺

It made me smile to know I was one of the first thoughts on her mind.

I texted back, *Good morning.* ☺

Getting ready 4 school now. Bye.

My face hurt from smiling. *Have a good day!* I responded.

My day was set from that point on. Haircuts came and went. I even twisted up a head of locs.

It was amazing to me how something so simple could make someone's day. On top of that, it was the result of a child. *My child.*

It was just so pure. She hit me up because she just wanted to say good morning. No ulterior motive, at least I hoped not. That was something special. At least it was to me.

After leaving the shop for the day, I stopped by Aldi's supermarket and went shopping for groceries. Whereas I had once been okay with the minute basics, I wanted to have more for when my daughter would be with me. I bought vegetables, meats, fruit, fruit punch, milk, soda, chips, cookies, spaghetti, macaroni, and whatever else I could think of that I thought she might like.

I couldn't remember ever seeing my cabinets and refrigerator so full. I wanted to be prepared even though I had no idea when she would be arriving.

After looking up a simple pasta recipe, I cooked my first real meal in my new place. I had only been there a little over a week, but I had already gotten settled in. I hadn't cooked anything other than some Ramen noodles and scrambled eggs since moving in, though. Otherwise, I was eating out.

Speaking of eating out, I hadn't had any company in a while, and I was overdue. I told myself that I would relieve some tension once I got settled, and now I didn't know how much freedom I would have once Lyric moved in.

I scrolled through my phone to see who might pique my interest. I shook my head as I looked over the names in my contact list. I couldn't find a single one that I wanted to share my first official dinner at home with.

I guess I was what some would call a social butterfly. After my breakup with Jordan, I had sworn off relationships. My feelings were way too important to me for me to risk giving them to somebody who didn't deserve them. So, I opted to keep my interactions cool and light. A fling here and there. It worked for me.

But, in that moment, while standing in my kitchen with a small pot of penne pasta and meat sauce, I realized it might have been nice to have a lady companion who I enjoyed enough to share this moment with. I wasn't looking for a relationship of great magnitude, but it hit me that I wouldn't even consider any of the women who I slept with as friends.

The thought was sobering.

I put the lid on the pasta and placed my first-time homemade garlic bread back in the oven.

I needed a beer.

I grabbed my keys and headed out the door to run to the corner store.

I heard the noise as I walked to my car.

"I want you gone!"

The statement wafted from an open window of my neighbor's house.

I was about to climb in my car, but curiosity got the best of me. I leaned against the door and listened.

"I was so fuckin' stupid-"

"Baby-"

"I'm not your baby! Your wife is!"

Ooh! I thought to myself with a wince.

It seemed my friendly neighbor turned out to be the side chick who was sick of her status.

For another minute, I listened to him trying to explain and her interrupting him before I heard glass break.

"Get the fuck outta my house!" I heard her yell.

I took that as my cue to get in my car and go. If she had screamed in pain or yelled to the point where I knew he was hurting her, I would've interceded, but it sounded like she had it under control, more or less. As I pulled out of my driveway, I glanced over at the house next door one more time.

Man, I really hope she has it under control.

I left and returned home in less than ten minutes. I pulled into my driveway at a snail's pace while trying to peek over in my neighbor's yard.

The car that I assumed was his was now gone. I saw the red glow from the tip of her cigarette as she took a puff while sitting on her front porch swing and looking at the setting sun. I climbed out of my car and glanced over at her briefly, debating on whether or not it would be appropriate to go over to check on her since we had never really spoken before. After taking another quick glance at her, I decided against it.

I could tell she was still pissed by the way her leg was shaking. I imagine she was trying to regain her composure, and I understood totally.

I threw my hand up to at least send her a quick, non-verbal greeting. She just looked at me and took another drag of her cigarette.

Refusing to be affected by the slight, I made my way to my front door and unlocked it. I had some pasta and garlic bread waiting to be enjoyed with one of the Heinekens that I had just purchased.

She can stay pissy, I thought to myself. *She shouldn't have been a side chick. Not my issue.*

But, I knew what was an issue. My growling stomach.

I entered the house and went straight to the kitchen to put

the six-pack minus one into the refrigerator. After fixing myself a plate of the pasta, I overloaded it with parmesan cheese and grabbed a piece of garlic bread out of the oven. Just as I was about to sit in front of the TV with my plate, the doorbell rang.

I went to answer the door, placing my food on the counter on my way.

Lo and behold, there she stood. After not receiving a response when I waved, I just looked at her.

"I'm sorry to bother you," she said without preamble, "but I was wondering if I could use your phone. I just broke mine."

I can only imagine how, I thought to myself, but instead, I replied, "Sure," then walked into the living room to get my cellphone off of the coffee table.

When I saw her still standing at the door, I told her, "You can come in. I don't want the house full of flies and mosquitos."

"My bad," she said, stepping inside and closing my front door.

While approaching her, I entered my security code to unlock my phone. After handing it to her, I went back into the kitchen to grab my plate and beer.

As I sat down on my sofa, I yelled out to her, "You don't have to stand at the door! You can come on in!"

She came further into the room but stopped at the dining table. I started in on my food as she placed her call.

"I'd like to place an order for carry-out," she spoke into the phone. Then, I heard her annoyance when she said, "Okay."

I chewed on a forkful of my pasta before asking, "Hold?"

She nodded and rolled her eyes. "I just wanna be able to

pick up my food and go back home. I'm not in the mood to wait and deal with the public this evening."

"Having a bad day, I'm guessing," I prompted.

"That's an understatement." She crossed her arms while still holding the phone to her ear. "Just realized I've wasted almost a year of my life on a liar."

"That sounds like fun," I commented before taking a swig of my beer.

"Tons," she replied dryly. Another two minutes passed before she spoke again. "My word! What's taking them so long? I just want to get a damn pizza and hole myself up in my bedroom! Is that too much to ask?"

"Yeah," I said after taking a bite of my garlic bread. "It's bad business keeping customers on hold for too long. I would've already hung up and found somewhere else."

"But their pizza is so good!" she responded enthusiastically. After a frustrated sigh, she hung up and walked over to me. "Thanks for letting me use your phone," she said, extending it to me.

"Did you wanna try to call somewhere else before you go?" I offered.

"Thank you, but that's okay. I'll just throw together a couple of peanut butter and jelly sandwiches."

She was heading to the front door when I stood up. "If you don't want to do that, you can take some of this pasta with you."

"I don't want to trouble you," she responded.

"It's no trouble," I told her as I made my way to the kitchen. "I made more than enough. Hell, I might've made too much."

"In that case, I'll take it," she said. "Thank you."

"At least that way you won't have to deal with a lot of

people," I added, pulling a plate out of the cabinet. "Do you like garlic bread?"

"Love it," she answered.

I grabbed two pieces out of the oven before spooning two heaps of pasta onto the plate.

"Is that enough?" I asked.

"Oh, that's plenty," she answered. "I really appreciate it."

"It's no problem." I grabbed the aluminum foil to cover the food. "I'd rather share it than let it go to waste."

"Makes sense," she responded. "Well, I'm glad I could benefit from your generosity."

"It's my pleasure," I told her before handing her the wrapped plate. "Bon appétit!"

I opened my fridge and grabbed another beer, holding it out to her. "I'm not sure if you drink, but it seems like you've had a rough day."

"I usually don't drink beer," she answered. "But, today, I'm more than willing to make an exception."

She accepted the bottle and, for the first time since the first time I saw her, gave me a big smile. I couldn't help but to smile back.

I walked her to the door and opened it for her.

"Thank you again," she said. Then, after stepping out onto my small porch, she turned around and looked at me. "I'm Melody King, by the way."

"No problem," I told her. "And I'm Jazz. Jazz Richardson."

"Well, it's nice to officially meet you, Jazz."

"It's nice to meet you, too, Melody. I hope your evening gets better."

She held up her plate and beer. "Well, this is a good start. Goodnight, Jazz."

"Goodnight, Melody."

I stood at the door and watched her sashay down my steps, then down my walkway. I couldn't help but to notice how her full hips swayed with each step. I could tell it wasn't deliberate. She moved fluidly. Even in her flat shoes, she almost floated as she walked. I wondered what she walked like in heels, because her movements dripped *sensual.* The irony is, I bet she didn't even know it.

As I sat back down to finish my plate, I pondered over a few things.

I admit that I usually found myself attracted to the trimmer women. I very seldom dated women above a size ten. Maybe it had been a subconscious choice. I don't know. I mean, I've seen many beautiful women who wore size 14 and up, and I always gave credit where credit was due. However, I'd never been intimate with one nor had a desire to be.

But, my new neighbor…

She was thick and wore it beautifully. Even casually dressed in her jeggings and powder blue tunic, she was appealing. Other than the lip gloss she wore, she was makeup free and still pretty as hell. She didn't give off a vibe of being artificial, at least from our first official meeting. Her semi-curly afro was pulled back with a scarf that matched her top. In spite of her mood, there was something about her that I found oddly refreshing.

Though we hadn't officially dined together, I was glad to have shared my first home-cooked meal with her. Even giving it to her to-go had pleased me more than the thought of dining with one of the options I had scrolled through my phone and rejected.

Still, she was my neighbor. So, whether I found her attractive or not, I made it a priority to never play where I stay. And she was way too close for comfort. Not to mention, she was *just* in some kind of relationship with a married man. No bueno.

But, she was definitely an option when it came to developing a friendship, and I was gradually starting to accept that I could use a few more of those.

RETURNING THE FAVOR

I slept in.

I knew I probably should've been at the shop, but I couldn't make myself get out of bed for anything. When my alarm went off, I hit the snooze button and rolled over. It wasn't until I heard my doorbell ring that I sat up. Groggily, I climbed out of bed and trudged to the front door.

"Who is it?" I yelled while approaching the door.

I heard her muffled reply as I looked through my peephole.

"Melody!"

I slowly inched the door open.

"Good morn- Oh, I'm sorry! Did I wake you?"

"It's cool," I told her, opening the door all the way. "I needed to get up anyway. I should've been at work already."

"Well, in that case, I'm glad I woke you." She smiled. "I wouldn't want you getting in trouble at work."

"I'm not going to get in trouble," I told her as I stepped back. "I make my own hours, and come and go as I please."

"That must be nice," she said, stepping inside. "What do you do?"

"I'm a barber," I replied, closing the door behind her.

"Oh, that's cool," she responded, touching the nape of her neck. "So that means you can hook me up and keep my kitchen clean back there when I need it, huh?"

I chuckled. "Sure."

I walked into the kitchen and grabbed a glass to pour myself some juice. "What can I do for you this morning?"

"I just wanted to bring your plate back before I headed out to run errands. I don't like holding on to other people's property for too long."

She held up the plate that I had given her the night before. "It's all nice and clean," she said as she handed it to me. "I appreciate it again. Much better than peanut butter and jelly."

"No problem," I told her. "It was just a little something I picked up online."

"Well, it was good. I owe you one."

"Okay," I replied while walking her back to the door. "I'm going to remember you said that."

"I mean it!" she said as I opened the door. "You have a good day, Jazz."

"You, too, Melody."

She gave a quick wave and descended from my porch.

I knew I would have to eventually stop watching her walk away, but this was not that day. When she was out of view, I shook my head and closed my door. Then, I finished my juice and jumped in the shower.

The shower refreshed me a bit. I had a little more pep in my step as I got dressed to go to the shop. After having another glass of juice, I grabbed my phone, keys, and wallet, then headed to my car. I was ready to go and make some money.

Or so I thought.

My first three clients went smoothly, but it was all downhill from there. By the time I started cutting my fourth client's head, shit started getting real. First, there was a small sneeze, then a cough, then another sneeze. Then, I started feeling woozy. When I nearly nicked my client, I knew I needed to take my ass home. I quickly finished up his cut and got my equipment together.

"I'm calling it a day," I said, looking at Dominique, one of the other barbers in the shop.

"You okay?" she asked. "It's not like you to leave so early, especially after coming in late."

"I know," I told her. "I'm just not feeling up to par."

"I think there's a bug going around, so yeah, you go home."

"Right," chimed in Rae, another barber. "I don't need you getting me sick and making me miss out on my money. Scram!"

I laughed and shook my head as I grabbed my bag and headed for the door.

Dominique, Rae, and I were pretty hot commodities. Out of the eight occupants in the shop, we were the only female barbers. There weren't too many in the immediate area, and we weren't gimmicks either. We were all good at what we did. We had all competed and participated in hair expos and had all come out on top. We had even been featured in a local magazine.

We had talked about venturing out and opening a shop of our own. Now with Lyric coming to live with me, I was putting even more thought into the notion. I think it would make her proud to have a mom who had her own business.

After getting in my car, I headed towards home. I stopped at a nearby convenience store to grab another bottle of orange juice so I wouldn't have to come out later to get some. As I walked to the front register, I nearly ran Melody over.

"Well, hey, neighbor," she said with a smile that

immediately turned into a look of concern. "Are you okay?"

"I'm okay. Just a little tired today. I took the rest of the day off, so I'm going to take it easy at home. Hopefully some sleep will make a difference."

"That's not a bad idea," she said with a nod. "You're looking a tad bit pale. Are you sure you aren't coming down with something?"

"I don't know," I told her. "I'm just going to try to sleep it off."

"Well," she began, "if you need anything, I will be right next door. Okay?"

"I appreciate that," I said, turning just in time to keep from sneezing in her face. "I'm so sorry."

"It's okay," she said with a chuckle. "You didn't get me. I should still be cootie free."

I chuckled a bit. "Well, let me go pay for this so I can go get my ass in the bed."

"Yeah, you do that," she said, nodding in agreement. "I'll swing by and check on you, if that's cool with you."

"Awww, you don't have to do that."

"I know I don't have to," she said, "but I believe in being a good neighbor. After all, you were so nice to me yesterday. The least I can do is check on you."

"Well, okay then. I look forward to it."

Maybe that wasn't the best response, but she gave me that ever-present smile anyway.

"I'll see you later then," she said. "Go home and take it easy."

"Will do."

She gave me a little finger wave before turning around to go search for whatever she had been looking for.

As I waited for my juice to be rung up, I looked back at

her as she reached for a drink in one of the coolers.

She sure is pretty. Too bad she's my neighbor.

After taking the short drive home, I went inside and immediately changed into a pair of sweatpants and an old t-shirt. It was barely hanging on by a thread, but it was so comfortable that I refused to get rid of it. After slipping on some house shoes, I went into the kitchen, poured myself a cup of orange juice, and downed it in three gulps. Then, I looked in the fridge and debated on whether or not I wanted to fix myself a plate of leftover pasta from the night before. After deciding against it, I closed the refrigerator door.

My appetite was almost non-existent. I knew I needed to eat something, but I just didn't feel up to it.

Looking at my trashcan, I saw it was reaching the limit. I figured I'd take it out before it had my kitchen smelling funny.

"You're supposed to be in bed!"

I looked up and saw Melody standing in her yard with her hand on her curvy hip.

"I know, I know," I said, holding my hands up in mock surrender. "I'm going. I just needed to take the trash out."

A cough caught me completely off guard, and I was embarrassed at the way I had to temporarily gasp to catch my breath.

"Are you one of those people who don't know how to just sit down and be sick?" she demanded.

"I'm not sick," I lied.

"Riiiight," she said, clearly not believing me. "Do I need to come over there and treat you like a baby?"

"I'll be fine," I told her, even though my throat was beginning to feel scratchy from the coughing fit I'd just had.

"Yeah, sure," she said, walking over to the wooden fence that separated our properties. "Girl, go in the house and lay your butt down. And leave the door unlocked so I can come and check on you."

"I'm from the hood," I told her. "We don't typically leave our houses wide open."

"It won't be wide open," she debated. As she walked away, she spoke loud enough for only me to hear. "The door will be unlocked. There's a difference. And look around. You are no longer in the hood. You'll be fine. Trust me this one time."

But I don't even know you, I thought to myself. However, after going back inside my house and closing the front door, I left it unlocked as she'd requested.

I grabbed a blanket out of one of my closets and a pillow off my bed and made my way back into the living room. I was leaving the door unlocked, but I damn sure wasn't going to leave my living room unattended.

I turned the TV on and found a movie on Netflix. Before long, I was asleep.

I sensed her arrival. Before she opened the door, I knew she was there.

"Come on in," I yelled, holding my head up slightly to make sure my voice carried to the door. I quickly laid it back down. It felt heavy as lead.

Yeah. I was sick as fuck.

"How did you know I was here?" Melody asked as she entered. "I hadn't even knocked or anything."

"I dunno," I answered from where I lay. "Intuition, I guess."

I watched as she came into the room. She sat a bag on the

table before approaching me and placing her wrist on my forehead.

"You're pretty warm," she told me. "I'm going to take a wild guess and say you have no intention of going to the hospital, right?"

"Right," I answered, burying myself further beneath my blanket.

"Well, I guess I'll just have to take care of you then."

She ignored my muffled protests as she turned around and went to grab the bag off of my dining room table. Then, she walked into my kitchen as if she couldn't hear me speaking, chattering along the way.

"It's apparent you aren't going to take care of yourself," she was saying. "So, you should consider it a blessing that you have me as your neighbor. And before you even think it, no, I'm not crazy. I just like to be nice, and since most of the people in this neighborhood are much older and it seems like you're here all by your lonesome, I figured you could probably use a friend around here as much as I could use one."

I lifted my blanket from around my face. "What makes you think I'm lonesome?" I asked as loudly as I could.

I heard her pilfering around in my kitchen, opening and closing cabinets and drawers before pausing to answer. When she peeked through the pass-through window between the kitchen and front of the house, she answered.

"Well, you've been here for weeks and I've only seen you with visitors once, and that was the day you moved in."

"Well, that's going to change soon," I yelled out before covering my face back up. "I won't be the only one here in the near future. A special lady will be here very soon."

She was quiet for a second.

I peered over the top of my blanket when she came into the living room and stood in front of me.

"I apologize," she said solemnly. "I didn't even think to ask if you had a mate. I didn't mean to step on any toes, and I don't want to cause any drama. I've had enough of that already-"

"Hold on a sec," I said, interrupting her. "You're not stepping on anyone's toes. I said a special lady, not a boo thang. There are no boo thangs coming in here."

"Oh, okay," she said, before turning and walking away. "I guess that means I can finish fixing you this soup."

She had barely made it back into the kitchen before my stomach started churning. As quickly as I could, I jumped up to run to my hall bathroom. I stumbled along my path, feeling as though the room was spinning. I made it to the toilet just in time to empty the contents of my stomach into it. I was amazed at how much came out of me considering I hadn't eaten all day. With closed eyes, I began to dry heave, and the feeling was worse than actually throwing up.

Feeling weak, I just wanted to lay back down. I blindly reached out and flushed the toilet. Afterwards, I closed the lid and sat on it.

Coolness came. I felt it against my forehead. At the same time, I felt a warm hand on my shoulder. I slowly opened my eyes and saw Melody standing there, her pretty face twisted in concern.

She firmly, but gently, dabbed my forehead and then the rest of my face with a few folded wet paper towels.

"I didn't know where you kept your towels," she said as she continued to nurse me. "So, I grabbed the next best thing."

I pointed toward the hallway. "They're in the closet," I

told her while turning my head away so the smell of my breath wouldn't hit her too hard.

"Here," she said, handing me a cup. "Rinse your mouth out while I get you a towel."

I took a swig of the warm salt water and swished it around in my mouth as she walked back into the hallway. Not quite ready to stand, I leaned over, threw the curtain back from the tub, and spit the saltwater into it.

She returned with a washcloth, wetting it and dabbing at my face again.

"Are you sure you don't wanna go to the ER?"

"I hate hospitals," I told her. "I try to stay away from them as much as possible."

"I see," she said, putting the washcloth on the sink. "Well, do you need help getting back into the living room?"

"I think I can handle it," I answered, rising slowly.

"Okay," she replied, though I could hear the doubt in her voice. "I'm going to go check on this food."

I stood upright as she exited the bathroom. After giving myself a moment to gain some kind of composure, I grabbed the washcloth from the counter and slowly walked to my bedroom. I peeked at myself in the mirror before going into the master bathroom.

Yeah, I look like shit, I thought to myself before grabbing my toothbrush.

I brushed my teeth and rinsed my mouth out with mouthwash before washing my face with a warm towel. I felt a little more sanitary as I trudged back to the living room. At least my breath no longer smelled like hot garbage.

I eased onto the sofa, sitting up to find something to watch. I settled for a *World's Dumbest* television show. It always tickled me to see stupid people pay for doing stupid shit. As I watched the stupidity of others being aired, the smell of something good filled the air.

Shortly after I had settled onto the couch, Melody came into the living room carrying a bowl and a coffee cup. She sat them on the coffee table in front of me.

"Here's a little chicken noodle soup that I threw together and a hot toddy. Drink it while it's still hot."

"Thank you," I told her, picking up the hot drink. I took a sip and tasted the lemon, honey, and liquor. It was strong, but it felt good going down my throat. I took a few sips, then a big swallow.

"Take your time with that," she warned. "It's pretty potent."

I scoffed and took another gulp of the hot concoction. "Girl, I can handle a little spiked hot tea."

It was almost four in the morning when I opened my eyes again. I sat up slowly and took in my surroundings.

Melody had stayed with me. She was curled up on the loveseat, her head propped up with one of the throw pillows I'd bought before moving. I hoped it wasn't the one I slobbered on that one time.

I moved my blanket and slowly brought myself to my feet. In spite of my body aching some, I was feeling a little better. I walked into my hallway and opened the closet door. After grabbing a throw blanket, I returned to the living room and covered Melody with it. I then padded into the kitchen, opened the fridge, and peered inside. My appetite was returning. I scanned several items before spotting the bowl she had brought to me earlier. I'd never even touched it. That damn toddy knocked me right out.

I put the bowl in the microwave and poured myself a glass

of juice. A minute or two later, I was back on the couch with my food and cold drink. I turned on the television, lowering the volume so it wouldn't wake my guest.

Instead of channel surfing, I watched her as she slept. I was curious about her. I admit that.

I mean, what kind of person takes care of a virtual stranger? Acts of kindness are rare these days.

After hearing her argument with who I assumed was her ex boo thang, I wondered what her story was. She seemed too sweet to be okay with being the other woman, but people are strange creatures sometimes. Was she really as nice as she came across? Or was this the calm before the crazy? I didn't have time for any psycho neighbors, especially with Lyric coming soon.

I was devouring the soup as she stirred and stretched. She slowly opened her eyes and looked in my direction.

"Hi," she said quietly. "How are you feeling?"

Despite sounding a little groggy, Melody's voice had taken on a sultry tone. It was sexy. For a quick moment, I wondered what she sounded like when she was being pleased. I shook the thought away and answered her.

"A little better. Thank you."

"I'm glad to hear it," she said, sitting up. "Is the soup okay?"

"This shit's the bomb," I answered before taking another spoonful into my mouth. "This ain't no ordinary chicken noodle soup."

"Yeah, I put my little twist on it," she replied, smiling proudly. "I added a few seasonings and a little heat to help clear up your system."

"Well, it's working like a charm," I told her.

"I'm glad," she said with a nod. She looked at me for a

moment before speaking again. "What's that on your wrist?"

I looked down at the tattoo that she was eyeballing.

I held it up for her to see. "It's a straight razor," I explained. "Ya know, the whole barber thing."

"I see now," she said, nodding once more and then looking at her watch. "Oh, I didn't realize it was so late. I need to go and check on my house. I think I left everything on. I hadn't planned on being here so long." She stood up and stretched again, then slipped on her shoes and looked down at me. "But, I'm glad I could help you out a little bit."

"And I truly appreciate it," I told her as I rose from the sofa to walk her to the door.

She turned around as I opened it. The look of concern on her face touched me.

"I will check on you later, but are you going to be okay for the rest of the night?"

"I think I'll be fine," I told her with a small smile. "Thanks to you."

"Well, that's what friends are for," she said, flashing me that sweet smile.

"Are we friends already?" I wanted to know.

She paused before stepping out onto the porch. "We will be."

It sounded like a promise.

I was cool with that.

"Goodnight, Jazz."

"Goodnight, Melody."

I watched as she walked back to her house. I didn't close my door until I saw her go inside. I made a mental note to get her number so I could make sure she was okay in instances like this. She didn't seem to have a problem looking out for me, so I would take a leap of faith and look out for her, as well.

I went back to the sofa, plopped down, and took a gulp of my juice. It was then that I noticed the piece of paper on my coffee table. I picked it up and read the small note from her telling me to call if I needed her, along with her number written on the bottom.

I smiled to myself.

I'm looking forward to giving this friendship a try.

THE FIRST DATE

The butterflies were back.

As I drove down the small highway, my stomach did flips. I don't know why I was so nervous. It wasn't like it was my first time with Lyric. However, it was the first time we would be out together, and I wanted it to be a good experience for her.

Maybe it was excitement more than nervousness that had my stomach flip-flopping as I turned on the street where they lived.

It was our first mother-daughter day.

Mother.

The terminology still did something to me.

Despite our daily interaction via text, it still seemed surreal that I was talking to my daughter. I still found myself repeating that I was a mom. For ten years, I'd kept it to myself, pushing it to the furthest regions of my mind and going about my everyday life.

But, that was all rapidly changing.

I was already prepping the room that I had planned on using as an office/workout/guestroom to become her bedroom. I bought paint that matched the paint in her bedroom at Mrs. Cross' house. I'd been surfing the web looking for a bedroom set, because I still didn't know whether or not hers would be coming to my house with her. I had even looked into childproofing the house until I reminded myself that she was a ten-year-old girl and not a toddler.

As I pulled up in front of the Cross' house, I took a deep breath to calm my nerves. "This is no different than when I go out with a chick. All I gotta do is relax and be myself." I laughed, then shook my head before scolding myself. "The fuck you mean, Jazz? This is *completely* different from going out with a chick. This is my fuckin' daughter."

But, I did follow my directive to relax.

After unfastening my seatbelt, I climbed out of my car. I bounced up the steps and took another calming breath before ringing the doorbell. Moments later, the door opened, and Mrs. Cross greeted me with a smile.

"Well, hello there, Jasmine," she said, stepping aside to let me in. "It's so good to see you again."

After closing the door behind us, she gave me a quick hug.

"Lyric!" she yelled. "Guess who's here!"

We both journeyed into the living room and sat down as Lyric came into the living room.

"Hey, Jazz!" she said happily. She came over to me and gave me a quick hug. "How are you?"

I smiled at how mature she sounded.

"I'm doing good, lil' mama," I replied with a grin. "How are you?"

"I'm great!" she replied enthusiastically.

"Are you done with your room?" Mrs. Cross asked her.

"Almost," she answered solemnly.

"Almost?" Mrs. Cross questioned. "Remember what I told you?"

"I can't go until my room is completely clean," Lyric

answered, looking at her. "All I have to do is vacuum."

"Well, hop to it," Mrs. Cross told her. "Jasmine is waiting on you."

"Yes, ma'am," Lyric replied before running to finish her chore.

I could easily see that Mrs. Cross didn't take no bullshit and kept Lyric flying a straight path. *Will I be able to do that?*

"What's the matter?" Mrs. Cross asked me. "Your whole face just changed."

"Nothing, really," I answered. Then, seeing her expression of disbelief, I admitted, "I'm still taking it all in. I mean, I see how you are with Lyric, and I don't know if I can come off the same way."

Mrs. Cross chuckled. "Honey, you're not supposed to. This is how *we've* raised her. I'm what some may call old school. This is how I was raised, and I've kept the tradition going."

"Well, I grew up in the system," I replied. "I was barely raised at all, and I don't want to put that on her."

"This is your opportunity to break a cycle before it can ever happen. You can be greater than those who were supposed to take care of you. They've already taught you what not to do, and you already know what that treatment feels like. I know you would never do that to Lyric. Otherwise, I wouldn't have called you. You can do this, Jasmine. I have faith in you."

The vote of confidence helped, but only a little.

"So what are you two going to do today?" she asked, changing the subject.

"I'm not sure," I answered. "I guess whatever she wants to do."

Mrs. Cross laughed. "I suggest you come up with a game

plan," she told me, shaking her head. "She will wear you out if you leave it up to her."

"See what I mean. I don't even know where to begin."

"It's a process," she replied. "You're not going to figure it all out in a day. Calm down. You'll get it." Her smile was soft as she changed the subject once more. "I know there's a movie that she's been wanting to see, so there's an idea for you. She also loves Monkey Joe's and walking around the mall with her little friends. As far as eating out, we try to steer clear of most fast food places, but pizza is always a winner."

"I'm ready!"

Lyric bounced into the room, gleefully approaching us.

"That was quick," Mrs. Cross acknowledged. "Did you do a good job?"

"Yes, ma'am," Lyric answered, nodding. "My room is super clean!"

"Good job," Mrs. Cross said, nodding approvingly. She then looked at me. "Are you ready?"

"As ready as I'll ever be!"

After catching a movie, I followed Mrs. Cross' suggestion and took Lyric to the indoor park with inflatable structures. I watched as she easily formed a quick friendship with another little girl. I sat back and watched as they played together, running from one side of the building to the other. After about an hour, she and her new friend ran up to me saying they were hungry.

They chattered away like they'd known each other for years instead of just an hour while they munched on the pizza that I ordered for them. I wondered if she and I would be able to communicate as easily.

After another hour of play, they got the okay from the

other girl's parents to exchange numbers before saying goodbye to each other. I watched the scene from where I sat, letting my apprehension win as I observed my daughter, who was obviously a people person. In Atlanta, I lived my life free and open with no fucks given about what folks thought of me.

But, now I had a daughter.

How would people treat her if they knew her mother was a lesbian? Some people can be so cruel. Would she be treated differently when folks found out her mom was a *big ol' dyke*? The thought of it scared me.

Can I take care of her without changing who I am?

In that very moment, I did something I didn't do often. I prayed.

I did it quietly in my mind. But, I did it.

Before taking her back to the Cross' house, we stopped at Stone Cold, where we sat and nibbled on custom-made ice cream while talking for a while. After chatting about things like favorite music and our mutual love for the color blue, she caught me off guard with her inquisitiveness.

"Are you nervous about being my mom?"

I tried to play it off that I had almost choked on my ice cream.

"What made you ask that, kiddo?"

"Well," she began, "I'm kinda nervous about being your daughter. So, I figured you might be nervous, too."

"You figured, huh?" I said with an amused nod.

I could tell that at age ten, she was already a bright girl, and it seemed she didn't have a problem saying what was on her mind.

"Well, why are you nervous?" I asked her.

"I've never been a daughter before," she replied with a

shrug.

She said it with such simplicity that it made my heart hurt for a moment. I knew how it felt to feel like I wasn't anybody's daughter, too, and it made me feel remorseful.

"What about the Crosses?" I asked, trying to steer my mind away from my guilt.

"They're my nana and pop," she answered as if it were the most obvious thing in the world and I was crazy for asking. "They love me and I love them, but I'm not their daughter. Now that I'm gonna be with you, I have to learn how to be a daughter."

She was too smart for *my* own good. I could tell already.

"Well, I'm gonna have to learn how to be a mom since I've never done this *mom* thing before either," I told her. "So, I think we're on a level playing field."

We ate our ice cream quietly for a moment.

"Well, I think you're going to be a good mom."

I smiled in surprise while looking at her. "Really?"

"Well, I hope so anyway," she continued, "because you are about to be stuck with me."

I chuckled and shook my head.

Too damn bright…

CONVERSATIONS & INVITATIONS

"Aye!" I said after opening my front door.

I couldn't stop the smile that crept on my face. It always made my day to see my best friend.

"What's goin' on wit'cha?" I asked, stepping aside.

"Not shit," JB said as she crossed the threshold to come inside my place. She took a look around. "I see it's all coming together, huh?"

"Yeah," I told her, closing the front door and following her into my living room. "I'm taking baby steps. It'll be right once I get it like I want it."

"True dat," she replied while sitting down on the loveseat.

"What brings you by?" I said before asking if she wanted a beer.

"Hell yeah," she answered. "Well, the girls are doing a 'girls' day out' kinda thing. Hair, nails, lunch, a movie and whatnot. I figured since it's Monday, you'd probably be at home. So, since we hadn't chopped it up in a bit, I thought I'd swing by."

"That's what up," I said, then went into the kitchen to grab a couple beers out of the refrigerator. I returned to the living room and passed the cold brew to my friend. "So what's new with you?" I asked, taking a seat on my couch.

"Not shit," she replied. "Different day, same hustle. Oh,

Nelle and I are helping with a charity event in a couple weeks. She made sure to set a couple of tickets aside for you. I left them at the house, though. I'll swing them by the barbershop later this week."

"What kind of event?" I wanted to know, cutting my eyes at my partner in crime. "It better not be some frou frou."

"It's a ball-"

"Awww, come on, man!" I interrupted. "You know I don't do that dressy shit!"

"Come on, Jazz," she chuckled. "It's for a good cause. We're raising money for this youth home. Hell, you don't even have to pay for your tickets. We already got you."

I looked at my friend closely. "Why do you want me there so bad?"

"Why can't I just want my ace to be there?" she asked, cutting her eyes back at me.

"Uh huh," I said, still eyeballing her. "There's something you ain't telling me."

"Nah," she countered, taking a swig from her bottle. "What's up on some Madden?"

"You ain't said shit," I told her, ready for the challenge. I grabbed the controllers for my game system and set it up for game play. "You ready for this ass whoopin'?"

She scoffed. "Puh-lease! Just don't take this ass whoopin' personally."

We were about ten minutes into the video game when my doorbell rang. I paused the game and bounced up to answer the door.

"Hey, neighbor!"

Her smile was as bright as the sun as she greeted me.

"Hey, Mel," I greeted her back, moving aside so she could step over the threshold. "What's up?" I asked while closing the door behind her.

"I'm about to head to the market and wanted to see if you needed me to grab anything for you while I was out."

"That is sweet of you-"

"Who's that?" JB asked from where she sat on the loveseat.

I could see her leaning over to try to get a better view of my guest. I rolled my eyes in amusement at my friend's nosiness before stepping further into the living room. "JB, this is my neighbor, Melody," I began as an introduction. "Mel, this is my best friend, JB."

"It's nice to meet you," Melody said, smiling and extending her hand towards my homie.

JB took Melody's hand into her own, shaking it slowly. "You have such a pretty smile, Melody."

I saw her brown cheeks flush, and I couldn't help but to cut my eyes at JB.

"Thank you," Melody nearly gushed.

"You're so welcome," JB replied with a smile before releasing Melody's hand.

"Yeah, JB came through while *her wife and daughter* are having a girls' day out," I informed Melody, suddenly feeling the need to explain.

"Oh, cool," Melody replied. She then turned her attention back to me. "So did you need anything?"

"A six-pack of Heineken, if they sell it," I answered as I reached into my back pocket to get the money to give her.

"Don't worry about it," she said, holding up her hand. "I got you on this one."

"You know you don't have to," I debated with her.

"I know," she said, walking back towards the door. "You can always return the favor later."

"And I will," I replied as I followed her to the door. "Thank you," I told her as I watched her step out onto my porch.

"You're welcome," she answered before turning to walk away.

I watched her for a moment before closing the door.

As I walked back into the living room, I caught the smirk on JB's face.

"What?" I demanded.

"Nothin'," JB said with a shrug, then casually added, "Nice neighbor."

"Uh huh," I said, side-eyeing her. "And what was that all about? *'You have such a pretty smile, Melody'*," I mimicked.

She chuckled. "Did that bother you?" she asked innocently. "I was just being friendly."

"Uh-huh," I countered. "I know your friendly, and you can't be friendly like that anymore, Lil' Mrs. Studsband."

"I am not being friendly *like that*," she answered with a full-blown laugh. "I am very happy with my wife and daughter."

"You better be," I replied, picking up my game controller to restart the game.

"So what's up with you and your friendly neighbor?" she then asked. "I saw your face when I spoke. Is she your new thing?"

"No, she is not my *new thing*," I answered, almost defensively.

"She's a little thicker than I'm used to seeing you with," JB continued as if I hadn't replied. "But, she is cute as hell. She had a nice ass booty, too."

"Really, dude?" I said, looking over at my friend.

She laughed harder, pausing the game. "Ooh! You like

her!" she exclaimed like she had just found a secret treasure.

"You're reading way too much into this," I told her. "We're just neighbors, and we are getting to know each other since we're probably the youngest cats in the neighborhood."

"Whatever you say," JB said, observing me closely. "Well, why don't you invite your neighbor to the fundraiser in a couple of weeks? Y'all could go as friends if you don't already have a date in mind."

"I haven't said I was going yet," I argued.

"The keyword is yet," JB threw back. "By the time Nelle talks to you, you'll go."

I rolled my eyes heavenwards. "Y'all get on my nerves," I told her. "I swear y'all do."

"We love you, too," she replied with a chuckle before returning her attention to my TV and unpausing the game. "Let me finish giving you this beatdown before you get in your feelings again about me making your crush blush."

"You know what? Fuck you," I shot back with a laugh, refocusing on the game. "For that, I'm really about to drag your ass."

"Well, come on, Cleetus! Come on!"

As the game ensued, I let my mind drift to my reaction to JB's mild flirtation with Melody. For that brief moment, I felt a little too territorial. I knew I needed to shake that shit off, though.

I shook my head at myself before refocusing on the game.

Besides, in a few days, a much more important lady will be in my life on a regular basis.

* * *

Those butterflies that had become regular guests in my stomach were back for a visit. I stood quietly as I waited nervously for the result of her assessment.

"I like it!"

I smiled and exhaled in relief as Lyric checked out her new bedroom for the first time.

She smiled and threw her small purse on her bed.

"Feel free to make yourself at home," I told her.

"Well, that's where I am, right?" she asked, still smiling.

"Yes, ma'am," I replied, smiling back at her.

I turned to where the Crosses were watching from the hallway. Then, I escorted them back into the living room so they could have a seat.

"This is very nice, Jasmine," Mrs. Cross said, nodding her head in approval.

"Well, it's not as nice and big as yours," I responded with a nervous smile, "but it's mine."

"And that's all that matters," Mr. Cross interjected.

"That's right," my former caseworker agreed. "It doesn't have to be a big sprawling house to be a nice one. It's small, but I think it's perfect for you and Lyric."

I nodded, acknowledging her comment. "I hope so," I confessed.

After a brief pause, she spoke again. "I am very proud of you and the woman you've become, Jasmine."

I felt my throat tighten as she continued.

"I always knew you had it in you to do something great. You just had to figure it out for yourself. And you have. Now it's time for a new experience in life. Being a mother. And I have faith you will also figure this all out."

I nodded, not trusting my voice at the moment.

"We will be here in town for the weekend if you need

anything," she informed me as she and her husband stood up. I followed suit. "We would stay longer, but we want you guys to get started on this new journey, and if we linger too long…" Her voice faltered.

"She's a little emotional about it," Mr. Cross stated with sincerity. "We know it's the right thing to do, but she's been in our lives since she was a baby, so it's going to take some getting used to."

She nodded and quietly sniffled.

Finally, I was able to speak. "She'll still be in your lives," I told them. "You guys are her grandparents. Always will be. And you will always be welcome here."

"That means a lot," Mrs. Cross responded with a soft smile.

I could see the moisture gathering in her eyes. She dabbed at them before regaining her composure.

"Well, let us go give her a hug and tell her bye."

"Not bye," I corrected. "Just 'see you later'."

"Right," she replied. "Thank you."

"No, ma'am," I told her. "Thank *you*."

I watched the bittersweet moment as the Crosses gave Lyric hugs and shared words of encouragement with the both of us. Lyric and I stood in the doorway and watched as they got in their SUV and drove away. We then looked at each other for a moment, both mentally trying to prepare for this next chapter of our lives.

A NEW CHAPTER

It was quiet for a moment as we watched the black SUV drive away. I looked down at Lyric as she continued to stare out the door. She looked like she was fighting back tears.

"You okay?" I asked.

My stomach churned as I waited for her reply.

"I'm okay," she answered after a couple of seconds. "I'm just going to miss them," she admitted.

"I know," I told her, "but you'll still be able to call them and stuff."

"Yeah, I know," she said quietly, then looked up at me. "You don't have to try to cheer me up. I'm really okay."

For a moment, there was silence. I cleared my throat before the silence became awkward.

"I saw you brought in some stuff. Do you need any help putting it up?"

"I think I'll be fine," she answered, seeming to snap out of her thoughts.

She started to walk towards her room but stopped before turning the corner. She gave me a small smile before speaking again.

"If I need any help, I'll let you know."

"Okay," I replied.

I watched as my daughter went into her bedroom.

Suddenly, my stomach fluttered and then took a dive as I stood in my dining area.

"I'm going to the bathroom," I yelled out. "I'll be back in a couple of minutes!"

"Okay!" Lyric yelled from her room.

I rushed to my bathroom, unsure of whether I needed to shit or throw up. I sat on my toilet for several minutes waiting for the feeling to subside. As it finally began to ease up, my doorbell rang. After quickly gathering my wits and washing my hands, I went and looked out of the peephole.

I couldn't help but to smile to myself as I spied on Melody, who was standing on my porch waiting patiently for me to open the door.

"Hey there," I greeted after opening it.

"Hey, yourself," she said with a smile.

Automatically, I stepped aside and let her in.

"What are you up to?" I asked her as we walked into the living room.

"Just checking on you, as usual," she answered. A noise from Lyric's room caught her attention. "I'm sorry. You have company-"

"Not necessarily," I interrupted. For a moment, I was hesitant. Then, I spoke out. "Lyric, come here for a minute, please."

Seconds felt like hours as I waited for her to enter the room.

"Yes, ma'am?" She paused as her gaze fell upon Melody. "Hello," she said with a wave.

"Hi," Melody replied with a friendly smile.

"Lyric, this is our neighbor, Mel," I informed my child before turning to Melody. "Mel, this is Lyric. My daughter."

Though she kept her game face on for the most part, her small gasp gave away her surprise. She walked over to my daughter and held out her hand.

"It's nice to meet you, Lyric," she said before my daughter accepted her hand in a polite handshake.

"It's nice to meet you, too, Miss Mel," she replied.

"No *Miss*," Melody corrected her. "Just *Mel*. Hopefully, we will be friends soon."

"That sounds nice," Lyric said, smiling up at our guest.

"How's your room coming along?" I asked her.

"I'm almost done," she answered. "I need some more hangers for the rest of my clothes, and I think I left my stand for my keyboard back at Nana and Pop's."

"Keyboard?" Melody chimed in. "As in electronic piano?"

"Yes, ma'am," Lyric answered with a nod. "I'm learning how to play the piano. My nana said I couldn't get a piano until I was older, but her and Pop got me a keyboard to practice on. I use my earbuds with it so nobody has to hear it when I practice."

I smiled at how my girl's eyes lit up as she talked about her instrument. I didn't even know she played the piano. We'd discussed that she liked music, but I hadn't known she liked it that much. I added piano lessons to my mental to-do list for her.

"I would love to see your keyboard," Melody told her.

When Lyric's smile stretched from ear to ear, I knew Melody had locked in her position as her newest friend.

"Follow me," Lyric instructed, almost skipping into her bedroom.

Melody sashayed behind her, and I pulled up in the rear.

The massive keyboard sat at the foot of her bed. She

pulled it towards the center of her bed and turned it on. Then, she flopped down onto the bed and began to proudly play simple tunes like "Mary had a Little Lamb" and "Yankee Doodle Dandy" before surprising me with Bob Marley's "One Love".

"How awesome!" Melody cooed and Lyric glowed from the praise. "Do you mind if I play something?"

"You know how to play?" Lyric asked in surprise.

"I sure do," Melody answered proudly.

I watched in amazement as Melody sat at the foot of Lyric's bed and turned the keyboard towards herself. I listened in delight as she easily strummed "Amazing Grace" before slipping effortlessly into John Legend's "All of Me". She finished off with Katy Perry's "Firework".

Lyric clapped as if she'd just been given a private concert by her favorite celebrity.

"You are so good," she gushed.

It was clear Melody now had a fan for life.

"Thank you," Melody replied. "So are you. And guess what?" she then offered once my daughter calmed down.

"Ma'am?" the youngster asked excitedly.

"I have a real piano at my house."

Lyric squealed in excitement. "Really?"

"Yep," Melody answered. "Maybe you can come and check it out sometime if your mom says it's okay."

My daughter looked up at me with hopeful eyes.

"That's cool with me," I told them, basically sealing the deal on their friendship and snagging a few brownie points for myself with the young'un.

"Thank you!" Lyric said happily, jumping up to give me a quick hug.

After the two ladies engaged in a few minutes of chit-chat while toying with the keyboard, Melody joined me back in the living room after Lyric put her earbuds in and began practicing on the black and white keys.

"So," Melody began, "is she the special lady that you had mentioned to me before?"

"The one and only," I answered as I flipped through channels on the television.

"I had no idea," she said, shaking her head in wonder.

"It's a long story," I told her.

"Well, maybe one day you will tell me about it."

I looked at her for a second. "Maybe."

"Uh huh." She smirked as she made herself comfortable on the loveseat. "I have a feeling you don't trust very easily."

"Don't take it personally," I responded with a mirthless chuckle. "I've experienced a few things in my life, so my trust is a hard-earned gift. I don't give it to many."

"Oh, I get it," she said. "You're not the only one who's had trust issues before. I just got out of a relationship with a married man, so…"

"What's the deal with that, anyway?" I wanted to know. "You don't strike me as side-chick material. I could be wrong, but-"

"I'm not," she said quickly. "I was just stupid, that's all." She took a deep breath and continued. "I knew he'd been married, but I thought he was divorced. He played me for almost a damn year."

"How do you deal with someone for almost a year and not know they're married?" I questioned. "Were there no signs?"

"No," she answered, irritation creeping into her voice. "He never wore a ring. We did everything that couples did.

We went on dates. He stayed the night sometimes. We went on weekend trips. Hell, he even introduced me to some of his friends and family. Just triflin'."

"So how did you find out he was still married?" I wanted to know.

"She confronted me one day after work," she answered with a sigh.

"Work?" I paused. "What do you do for a living?" I asked when it dawned on me that I never asked her before.

"A little of this, a little of that," she answered with a chuckle. "Seriously, I'm a receptionist at my aunt's law firm. I also give private piano lessons."

"So you're that good on the piano?" I queried.

"Yeah," she replied with a soft nod. "I'm that good. I love music."

"I think you're going to become Lyric's new best friend," I told her. "I can't have you upstaging me this early in the game."

"She's a cute kid," Melody said. "I like her already."

I grinned like a proud parent. "Yeah, she something else. But enough about her for a minute. I wanna know what happened with ol' boy's wife."

She took a deep breath and continued. "She came to my job. She tried to get real fly with me. She said she's known about me since the beginning, and it was only a matter of time before he would come back home. He always did, she'd said. I was all kinds of whores and sluts, let her tell it. I think I handled it well. I told her that I didn't know anything about her and that I thought he was divorced. Then I gave her my aunt's business card and told her that she might need to use it if she ever needed a divorce lawyer. She was livid."

I laughed. "Oh, that was slick! Very nice!"

"Yeah, I played it off," she replied, "but I was embarrassed as hell. We had a new client in the office, and they witnessed the whole thing. But, more than that, I felt so stupid. I shut that shit down that same evening. He played me so good, but I wasn't about to let him keep playing me."

"Well, you're better off without him," I told her.

"Oh, I know," she said with a snort. "It's definitely his loss. My feelings were hurt for a second and I was pissed about wasting almost a year of my life, but I'm okay. I started back smoking since then, though. After quitting for three years, I let him stress me out like that."

She shook her head in disgust.

"Well, you quit once," I told her. "You can stop again."

"True," she agreed with a nod. She then looked at me as if something suddenly occurred to her. "Guess what I just did?" she said with excitement.

"What?" I asked, curious.

"I just shared a part of myself with you!" she stated with mock astonishment. "See how easy that was!"

I chuckled. "Very funny. Be patient with me. Sharing is something that's kinda new to me. But, if it makes you feel better, you're the first person to meet my daughter."

"I'll take that," she replied. "That's definitely a big deal."

We sat in comfortable silence for a minute before I spoke again. "I was going to take Lyric out for pizza in a little bit. You're welcome to join us."

"I'd love to."

An hour later, we were in Stockbridge dining at Stevi B's Pizza Buffet. We went back and forth between eating from the buffet and playing games in the game area. As I sat and watched my neighbor – who was slowly becoming my friend – interacting and laughing with my daughter, I thought about how we might just be fortunate to have her around.

The more I thought about it, the more I liked it.

And that shit scared me a little.

GETTING THE HANG OF THINGS

I admit it. The first few days were a little bumpy.

After all the preparing I had done for Lyric to come live with me, I had basically forgotten to arrange care for her while I was working. I ended up having to take a few days off from work to get that situated. After getting some advice from Mrs. Cross, I found a summer program to enroll her in. I immediately figured out that childcare wasn't going to be cheap. I had already begun planning my work schedule in my head so I could be off by the time she got out of school.

I didn't like having to pay the enrollment fee for getting her into a program, but I was glad to even be able to get her in since it had already started. She had only been living with me a couple days, and I was already getting some Parenting 101.

Lesson number 1: Activities for kids ain't cheap.

Lesson number 2: Plan ahead.

Other than those lessons learned, by the end of the first week, we began to fall into our own routine. I would drop her off, go to work, get off by four, pick her up, and then we'd decide on dinner. We chatted while we ate, mostly small talk. She spent most of her time in her room either playing on her keyboard or her tablet. By nine o'clock, she'd had her bath and was usually in bed asleep.

I was still adapting to her being with me, so I didn't push for too much extra conversation. I remembered how I didn't want to be bothered when I went to a new place. I thought maybe she felt the same way.

Melody had become an even more regular staple in the house. She checked on us every day. Sometimes she would go in the room and play the keyboard with Lyric. I think they talked more with each other than either of them did with me. Sometimes I was grateful for it, and sometimes I didn't know how to feel about it.

I was tempted to tell JB about it when she came into the shop to get her hair twisted one morning, but I wasn't quite ready yet. Instead, I let her entertain me with her own tales of parenthood, marriage, and her life in general. She reminded me about her parents' upcoming anniversary get-together before attempting to slide into my personal business.

"So are you going to bring your new boo thang – I mean, neighbor to my folk's get-together or what?" she wanted to know.

"First of all, she is not my boo thang," I corrected. "She's just a friend, and I don't know who I'm bringing to your folk's shindig."

"Well, what about the fundraiser this weekend?" she interrogated. "Are you bringing her to that?"

"Is that this weekend?" I asked, trying to change the subject as I palm-rolled one of her locs. "I'd forgotten all about it!"

"Well, this is your friendly reminder," she shot back. "As a matter of fact, I have the tickets in the car. I'll give them to you before I leave."

I rolled my eyes, but chuckled to myself. "I still think something is up. You want me to go too bad for there not to be."

"I'm innocent," she said, holding her hands up in mock surrender. "It's all Nelle's idea."

I paused and looked down at my friend. "*What* is all Nelle's idea?"

After a quick moment of hesitation, she replied, "For you to come!"

"Uh huh," I replied with a look of skepticism as I continued twisting her hair.

Something was up. I just didn't have a damn clue what.

"Are you nervous?"

I looked at my daughter as she glanced at me while playing a game on her cell phone.

"Nervous about what?"

"Asking Mel out on a date."

I shook my head in surprise. "What makes you think I'm going to ask Mel out on a date?"

"I saw the tickets on the kitchen counter," she answered. "They said the doors open at seven and the festivities start at eight, and since my bedtime is nine, I figured the tickets were for the two of you."

"You just figured, huh?" I asked, amused. "Well, Penny, what else have you figured out?"

"Penny?" she asked, looking at me with confusion on her face.

"The girl from Inspector Gadget, *his niece," I explained. "The one who really solved the crimes. With her dog, Brain."*

She looked at me blankly.

"You don't know who Inspector Gadget is?" I asked incredulously. After witnessing her nonchalant shrug, I dramatically clutched my pearls. "What kind of childhood have you been living?"

For a minute, our previous conversation went forgotten as I got up to go into the kitchen to check on the chicken casserole I had put in the oven. After making sure it was ready, I slid a baking sheet filled with garlic buttered biscuits in the oven.

The doorbell rang, interrupting my process. I had already assumed who my visitor was, but I looked through the peephole anyway. She stood there with her hands clasped behind her back, looking as pretty as ever. For the thousandth time, I wondered to myself, *Why does she have to be so damn pretty?*

I shoved the thought to the back of my mind as I opened the door.

"Hey, Mel," I said, smiling as I stepped aside to let her in.

"Hey, Jazz," she said, smiling back at me as she walked by.

"Mel!"

I watched my daughter jump up and run to give Melody a hug as if it had been years since she'd seen her. For a moment, I was a little jealous. I mean, she hugged me sometimes, but never quite like I had seen her hug Melody. I wanted those kinds of hugs.

"Hey, girlie," Melody said, enjoying my daughter's embrace. "How was your day?"

"It was okay," she answered cheerfully.

I watched her take Melody by the hand and begin to pull her towards her room.

"I practiced the song you showed me," she told her proudly. "I can't wait to play it for you!"

"Okay," Mel said with a chuckle, following my daughter's lead.

I shook my head and made my way back into the kitchen. After grabbing a beer out of the fridge, I popped it open, leaned against the counter, and took a swig as I listened to the music from Lyric's keyboard drifting through the air. I could hear as Mel praised her and also helped her with what she could improve on.

At that moment, I decided I would ask her about officially giving Lyric lessons. But, first, I had a request of my own.

"Hey, Mel," I called out. "Can I borrow you for a minute?"

A minute later, she came into the kitchen.

"What's up?" she asked, leaning against the doorjamb.

"Are you trying to steal my daughter away from me?" I half-joked, trying to break the ice.

"Never that," she answered with a chuckle. "She's a cute kid. She makes me smile, and she's smart as hell."

"I can't argue with you about that," I replied, then cleared my throat before speaking again.

Was I really nervous? I had asked plenty of women out without a moment of hesitation. But, I couldn't deny the quick flutter of butterflies in my stomach as I opened my mouth to speak.

"I got a question for you," I finally said.

She looked at me with curiosity written across her face.

"I have this little thing I'm going to this Saturday. It's kinda formal, I think. I was wondering if you were free to go with me – just as friends, of course."

Her response was quick.

"I would love to," she began with a smile, "but I already

have a prior engagement this Saturday. I'm sorry."

For a moment, she looked sincerely sorry.

"It's no big deal," I said quickly, trying to play it off. I'd be lying if I said her friendly rejection didn't bruise my ego a bit. "I just figured I'd ask."

"I would love for us to do something together, though," she admitted. She smiled and added, "As friends, of course."

I had to smile a little. *Is she mocking me?*

"Can I take a raincheck?" she asked. "I'll make it up to you."

"That's cool," I told her, trying again to sound nonchalant. "Dinner is almost ready," I informed her, changing the subject. "You know you're welcome to join us."

"I would like that very much," she replied. "What's on the menu?"

I pulled an extra plate out of the cabinet and checked on the biscuits as I told her what was for dinner. She returned to Lyric's room to continue fiddling around on the keyboard with her while I fixed our plates.

I tried not to let her rejection bother me. I mean, how could I be mad because she had already made other plans? There were a number of women I could call who would be happy to go out with me.

But, I couldn't think of a single one *I* wanted to accompany me.

After a pleasant dinner, we all watched a movie before Lyric excused herself to go take her bath. While she bathed, I escorted Melody to the door and she thanked me for a great dinner.

"My pleasure," I told her as I opened the door to let her out.

After crossing the threshold, she stopped, turned around, and looked at me thoughtfully for a moment.

"I really enjoy spending time with you two," she expressed quietly.

I didn't know what I was expecting, but it hadn't been that.

After a quick second, I replied, "We enjoy you, too, Mel. We really do."

For a moment, neither one of us spoke. We just glanced at each other. I was rooted where I stood. She seemed stuck, too.

"Well," she said suddenly, pulling me out of my temporary bind, "goodnight, Jazz."

"Goodnight, Mel."

I watched her until she made it to her porch and went inside her house. After I closed my front door and locked it, I wondered what the hell had just happened.

Had there been a little tension in the air? A little electricity maybe? Or maybe it was just in my head because I hadn't gotten laid in what felt like a month of Sundays.

The thought of getting laid brought me back to my current dilemma. I still didn't have a date for the event on Saturday.

And I still couldn't think of anyone who I would want to take.

I heard Lyric come out of the bathroom and go into her bedroom. I gave her a couple of minutes to get settled before going into her room to tell her goodnight.

As I was about to walk back out of her room, a thought occurred to me. I turned around and looked down at her.

"Hey, Lyric," I said to her suddenly.

"Ma'am?" she answered in the middle of a yawn.

"Wanna stay up past your bedtime this Saturday?"
Her smile was all the answer I needed.

PLEASANT SURPRISES

She looked like a little princess.

I smiled as I leaned against the doorway to her bedroom and watched her twirl in front of the mirror for the umpteenth time.

Though we had been out on many occasions, this would be my first time introducing her to the world as my daughter, and I wanted her to feel special and pretty. From the look on her face, I hit the mark.

It had only taken us about fifteen minutes to find the perfect dress with matching shoes for her. It was royal blue, satiny, and matched the blue of the linen pants and sports jacket that had been hanging in my closet for a while. On the flipside, it took me almost three hours to shampoo her hair in our kitchen sink, detangle that massive shit, blow it out, and flat iron it. I had to reach way back in my memory to remember what it would take to handle her hair.

I immediately wished I had just taken her to a salon. I was used to doing haircuts and the occasional braiding and locs. I hadn't needed to pick up a damn flat iron in years. I debated on whether I would ever do her hair again.

Seeing her giggle and smile at her spiral curls in the mirror made it all worthwhile, though.

After getting her altogether, I jumped in the shower and

got myself ready for our evening out. I took in my appearance in the mirror. I was fresh from my freshly tapered cut to my blue suit, to my crisp white button-up, down to my Kenneth Cole dress shoes. After splashing on a little cologne, I was ready to go.

I walked into the living room and found Lyric sitting on the couch playing a game on her phone. She looked up at me and smiled.

"You look pretty," she complimented.

"Pretty?" I laughed. "I can't remember anyone calling me pretty before. I've been called handsome but never pretty. At least I can't remember it."

"Why not?" she asked, standing up and cocking her head over in thought.

"I guess because pretty is so – I dunno – girly."

"But you're a girl," she reasoned with simplicity in her tone. "Even if you have a haircut like a boy and dress like a boy, you're still a girl, and I think you look pretty."

For a moment, I was humbled. I think I even felt my face get a little warm.

"Well, thank you," I told her. "I'm glad you think I'm pretty. But, I'm not nearly as pretty as you are."

She twirled around, eating up the compliment. "I know, right?"

I laughed at the touch of cockiness. Yes, she was definitely my child. That kind of confidence had to be hereditary.

Enjoying the moment, I pulled out my phone. "Let's get a pic before we go!"

She bounced over to me and put on a pretty face, and we took a quick "selfie" picture. Still basking in the moment, I uploaded it to my phone app and posted, *Taking this little lady out for a night on the town. She says I'm pretty.* I followed the text with a smiley face.

I knew there was about to be a flood of comments when the picture hit the airwaves.

"Ready to go?" I asked her, holding my arm out to her.

"Yes, ma'am," she answered, linking her arm with mine.

We hadn't even made it to the car before I got the first notification on my phone. I ignored it as I started the car. We were off to our first major appearance as mother and daughter.

The Mansion Elan had been transformed from a hot club to a beautiful ballroom. Everything sparkled. Tables had been set up for patrons to enjoy finger foods and small desserts. The bars were open, serving everything from virgin drinks to Long Island Iced Tea. A catwalk had been assembled that stretched to nearly the center of what was usually the dancefloor.

Lyric looked around the building in awe of the sights. I smiled to myself as she wiggled a little to the music the deejay had going.

I escorted her to the bar where a pretty bartender waited, dressed in black and white with a black bowtie.

"Good evening, ma'am," she said, addressing Lyric. "May I see your wristband?" she asked with a smile.

"They said the wristbands are for people over twenty-one," Lyric answered. "I have some years to go."

The bartender laughed. "Oh, I thought you were just a tiny woman," she joked.

"Not yet," Lyric replied. "But, I'm on my way!"

After snickering at the exchange between the two, I ordered Lyric a Shirley Temple. After debating with myself on what I would drink, I opted for the same since I would be driving back home with my kid in the car.

As we walked around, my daughter chattered excitedly while pointing out all of the dresses that amazed her. She told me that she had never been to anything like this.

"Well, I went to a school dance once, but this is way bigger," she admitted enthusiastically.

I chuckled. "Well, yeah, I imagine this is a little bit grander."

I was tickled by her excitement. I think she talked more in the short time we had been there than we had all week. I was enjoying it. It was refreshing for me. To see her eyes lit up gave me a bit more hope that I would be able to do this whole "mom" thing.

"Mel!"

I looked up after my daughter shouted with glee. She took off running to the one person who could always steal her attention from me. Normally, I would feel a grain of envy at my kid's adoration of our neighbor, but tonight, I felt something else.

I paused where I stood, frozen for a moment.

She was beautiful.

The black cocktail dress she wore hugged her curves, baring her shoulders and a set of legs that instantly grabbed my attention. For a brief second, I wondered what they would feel like on my shoulders, but I shook the thought away as my gaze fell upon her face.

Her usual barely-there make-up had been replaced with a full-out glam look. Her hair had been silk pressed and fell past her shoulders in big waves. Those usually gloss-covered lips were now protected by a mahogany hued lipstick, and it called to me. I saw her lips part a little as if she'd gasped. It was then that I noticed she was checking me out, too.

Regaining my decorum, I walked over to her.

"Well, hello, neighbor," she said with a smile that almost seemed shy.

"Well, hello to you," I responded back. "You look amazing."

I could've sworn she blushed.

"Thank you," she replied. "So do you."

"We all look great!" Lyric chimed in, lightening the moment.

"Yes, we do," Melody agreed, laughing.

"She's a little cocky," I said with a smile. "I don't know where she gets it from."

"Uh-huh," Melody mocked. "Where are you guys sitting?" she asked.

"I have no idea," I answered. "I need to find my friend and see what's going on. Her wife is a part of this whole shindig. We just got dressed and showed up. I'm surprised to see you here, though. But, now, I don't feel so bad about you turning me down."

"At least now you know it was for a good reason." She smiled. "And I'm still gonna make it up to you."

"And I'm still going to hold you to that," I told her.

For a minute, neither of us spoke. It was Lyric who saved the day again.

"I'm so happy to see you," she told Melody. "I'm so surprised."

Then she put me on blast.

"I think my mom was a little sad when you said you couldn't come with her."

I looked out at the crowd, unable to make eye contact. Once more, I made a mental note. This time, as a reminder to teach her how to be a little more tactful.

"But, you know what?" she continued. "My nana told me that everything happens for a reason. And if you had said yes, *I* wouldn't be here. Then we wouldn't all be here together."

Nice save, little girl.

I looked back at Melody and found her smiling at my daughter.

"Now that's a wonderful way of looking at it."

"I think so, too," I chimed in, looking at the both of them.

Lyric smiled proudly at me about her shared epiphany before turning back to Melody and asking, "When we find a table, will you come sit with us?"

"Maybe," she answered.

"Unless you came with a date already," I threw in.

At that moment, the possibility of her not coming alone hit me, and I didn't care for how it made me feel.

"No," she replied. "I'm solo. But, I'm actually here working tonight, so it may be a while before I'm free to even sit down."

"Working? What kind of work are you doing?" my daughter inquired.

"It's a surprise," she replied, taking a couple steps back. Her smile mirrored the Mona Lisa. "You'll see very soon."

"We look forward to it," I told her as she turned to sashay away.

Jesus! That dress was hugging her in all the right places. I'd never been jealous of an item of clothing before, but there's a first time for everything.

I then looked at my daughter. "You didn't have to put me on blast, ya know? Telling her I was sad and whatnot."

"But you were," she debated as we started moving around.

"I wasn't sad," I countered. "I was disappointed."

"Isn't that the same thing?" she wanted to know.

"Not always," I replied, shaking my head, amused by her inquisitiveness. "Let's go find my friend."

As we walked around, I saw a few familiar faces, some belonging to women I had gone out with before. Their expressions varied from smiles of those who I had positive partings with to eyerolls from a few that didn't end so well. There were even a few glances that looked like they were curious about the young lady who was with me. I took it all in stride and kept it moving until I finally found JB at one of the other bars in the room.

"Finally!" I voiced with satisfaction. "We've been walking all over this place trying to find you!"

"What up, though?" she said cheerfully, giving me dap. "For a minute, I didn't think you were coming."

"I wasn't gonna let you down," I told her. "And I know Nelle wouldn't let me live it down if I *didn't* show up."

"You already know."

We both chuckled for a second before I saw JB's expression change to one of curiosity as she looked slightly behind me.

"So, um, who's your little date?"

I moved Lyric to stand in front of me.

"Lyric, this is my best friend, JB."

She held out her hand to shake my friend's. "It's nice to meet you, Miss JB."

JB snorted in amusement. "*Miss*? Just call me JB, okay, kid? And you are…?"

"I'm Lyric," she said simply, as if that explained everything.

My friend looked up at me, waiting.

"This is Lyric," I said, suddenly feeling a little nervous. After taking a quick breath, I continued. "My daughter."

For a moment, JB said nothing. My stomach churned a little as I waited for her response.

She laughed. "No, really. Who is she?"

"She's my daughter," I replied.

"Like from an ex?" JB asked. "You got custody of one and didn't tell me?"

"No," I said, trapped somewhere between exasperation and amusement. "Like I gave birth to her. Like we have the same DNA. Like look at her, then look at me."

I watched my friend look back and forth between us. I watched her eyes widen in disbelief.

"Well, I'll be damn- My bad, little girl."

"It's okay," Lyric assured her. "I've heard curse words before."

JB chuckled and shook her head. Then, she looked at me. "We've been aces for how many years now? How did I not know you had a whole kid?"

"It's a long story," I replied. "We'll have to sit down with a few beers, and I'll tell you about it."

"Soon, bruh," my friend replied.

"Okay," I told her.

I knew I had just pulled the rug from under her, but hell, the rug had been pulled from under me, too.

"So do you have any idea where we're supposed to be sitting?" I asked, changing the current topic.

"You already know," JB said, smiling eagerly. "Only VIP for my fam. Come on, I'll show you to our table."

We followed JB to a table that was along the left side of the catwalk. In the middle of it was a card that said "Reserved". At the other nearby tables, patrons sat sipping on drinks and sampling hors d'oeuvres, ready for the fundraiser to begin.

JB excused herself, telling us that she would be back after making sure Shanelle was good to go.

As I sat down, I noticed my realtor sitting at the table, as well, with a bad-ass looking chick next to her.

"Well, hello there, Joi!" I said with a huge grin. "How have you been?"

"I've been great," she answered, smiling. "How are you enjoying your new home?"

"I'm loving it," I told her enthusiastically. "I ended up changing that extra bedroom into a room for my daughter."

"Your daughter?" she asked, her surprise evident. "Is this lovely young lady your daughter?"

"Yes, ma'am," Lyric beamed, happy to be called a lovely young lady.

"Lyric, this is Ms. McIntosh," I introduced. "She sold me our house."

"Thank you, Ms. McIntosh. I love our house," Lyric told her.

I could almost see her pocketing the heart she'd just stolen from Joi.

"You are so welcome," Joi nearly gushed. Then, she cleared her throat. "Forgive my rudeness, Jazz. This is my wife, Toya."

I stood up so I could reach over to shake her hand. "It's nice to meet you," I told her. I then looked over at Joi and gave her an exaggerated thumbs-up.

Her wife was fine as fuck.

They both laughed, and Joi seemed to glow a little at my unspoken compliment.

If she hadn't mentioned her before when I was in the process of getting my house, I wouldn't have ever guessed she was married to another woman. Hell, Joi was kind of fine her damn self.

I was curious to know what their story was but knew it was none of my business.

We made small talk around the table. JB soon joined us.

"Everybody doing okay?" she asked, taking a seat next to me. After a few words of confirmation, she continued, "Nelle will be with us shortly. She's about to get the show started."

Almost as if on cue, the music changed and Shanelle stepped out from behind the curtain, striking a pose that screamed "Boss Diva". She gave the crowd a moment to give her their attention, before strutting down the catwalk and stopping at the end. She then struck a pose and gave a fierce face, showing off the beautiful pink maxi-styled skirt with matching crop top and green accessories, paying homage to her college sorority. The designer managed to make the outfit look both flashy and elegant.

Shanelle then turned around and strutted back down the catwalk towards the stage. She stopped again and struck one last fierce pose before performing a couple of vogues. Then she laughed and signaled for the deejay to turn the music down.

"Good evening, everybody," she began once the chatter lessened. "First, I want to thank all of you for coming out to show your support. It means the world to me and the kids that we are doing this for.

"Before we get started, I want to share something with you," Shanelle continued. "Many of you may know me from business and from the community services we do throughout the year, and some of you are friends of mine from college. When I was in college, it looked like I had it all together. In the public eye, I was Miss Thang, but what most didn't know is that I was going through a personal struggle. You see, I met this fantastic woman and fell head over heels in love with her. But, always being in the public eye, I was torn between being who everyone thought I was and being who I wanted to be. When I finally found the courage to walk in my truth, it wasn't an easy journey. My family didn't want to accept it. They even went as far as to get our church pastor involved. Shortly after that, my father came around, but it took almost two years before my mother and I were even in the same room with each other. She surprised me and was sitting in the front row on the day I became Mrs. Shanelle Carter-Donovan. It took a while, but we were finally able to get back on track. I was very fortunate, but I realized there are so many people who aren't as lucky as I was. Quite a few of them are our city's youth. That's why this project has been so important to me. Some of these kids and young adults will never have the opportunity that many of us have had. Some are in bad living situations. Many are homeless and runaways. They don't have anywhere to go or anyone to turn to. And honestly, in a city like Atlanta, that should never be an issue.

"That's why we are here tonight. We're here to make sure they have a place to go. We've already secured two buildings — one in Decatur and one in Jonesboro, and we are working on securing another one as well as rehabilitating several houses. Each large facility will provide room and board for thirty youth and young adults. They will have access to food, hot showers, a place to sleep. A nurse and a counselor will be on site. They will be able to get assistance with finding a job or getting their GED or even return to public schooling. They need more than these streets…"

As I listened to my friend speak so passionately, I remembered that at one point, I was one of those kids. For a moment, my throat tightened up. I mentally made a note to contribute in any way that I could. I returned my full attention to the stage.

"...Tonight's fundraiser will feature two auctions," Shanelle was saying. "One will be a silent auction for the wonderful clothes being featured in tonight's fashion show. Miss Terrisa Joi, creator at Strawberrykiss Designs, is also a technical sewing specialist at Art College. She and her team have put together some amazing designs just for this event. All proceeds from the silent auction will go towards necessities for the facilities.

"Our Date Night auction will follow the fashion show, and bidding for the clothing auction will take place right after. Thank each and every one of you for your roles in ensuring that this venture will be a success. Now, let's get this show started!"

Lyric and I clapped with the rest of the crowd as the music picked up and lights flashed to the beat. We watched in delight as the models, both male and female, slim and full-figured, showcased the various designs created by the designer and her team.

I was surprised when Melody strutted down the catwalk, throwing those hips from left to right. She paused halfway, flashed us a smile, and winked.

Lyric screamed in excitement; I clapped in awe.

How did she get so fucking fine?

Why did she have to be my friend?

And just when I thought it was over, she surprised me again.

HER BIGGEST FAN

"We hope you all enjoyed the fashion segment," Shanelle said into the mic, addressing the crowd after the awesome display of designer creations. "Bidding for the silent auction will start shortly. Right now, we'll have a brief intermission before we begin our Date Night auction. Please feel free to refill your drinks at the bar or catch members of our wait staff as they go by, and don't forget to ask them about the delicious hors d'oeuvres, as well. For your listening pleasure during the intermission, we have a special guest who was also one of the lovely models for tonight's event. Ladies and gentlemen, please give a round of applause for the phenomenal Miss Melody King."

The audience clapped loudly as I sat transfixed on her.

She stood on the stage with nothing but a microphone in front of her.

Completely spellbound, I watched as she started off her set with her version of Ledisi's "Alright". I was blown away when she switched it up and performed the 70's jam "Tell Me Something Good". And I was turned the hell on when she gave a sultry rendition of Jill Scott's "Come See Me".

As she performed that last song, our eyes locked for a minute, and I was willing to bet my soul she was singing it to me. I'm sure others felt the same as she glanced over the crowd during her performance.

She was a natural. She sang as if she'd been born with a microphone in her hand. She was confident; she looked relaxed. She looked sexy as hell, and the image of her on that stage had been burned into my mind.

I figured she was a pretty good musician by the way she tinkered around with Lyric's keyboard, but I really had no idea how talented she was. In a matter of minutes, I had become her biggest fan.

The "playboi" in me now yearned to know what she sounded like when she moaned.

I shook my head at myself. She was making it harder for me to want to remain platonic with her.

"She's so good!" Lyric chimed in after the set ended. "I didn't know she could sing like that!"

"Neither did I," I replied, still in awe.

"Your neighbor there has a nice set of pipes on her," JB said, smirking at my expression.

"Why didn't you tell me that she was performing?" I asked.

"Hell, I didn't know until yesterday," she answered. "Nelle handled all of that."

"Nelle handled all of what?"

I looked up as Shanelle approached the table.

"The entertainment," JB answered before meeting her halfway for a quick kiss.

"Oh," she answered before turning her gaze towards me. "So, um…somebody has been holding out."

"It's not like that, sis-"

"Don't 'sis' me," Shanelle interrupted. "It's exactly like that, but I'll tell you off later. For now, introductions please."

I shook my head in chagrin and amusement before

speaking again. "Shanelle, this is my daughter, Lyric. Lyric, this is-"

"Your auntie Nelle!" Shanelle jumped in excitedly, reaching out and pulling Lyric in for a big hug. "You are so freakin' pretty, girl! That melanin is poppin'! Do you like getting your hair and nails done? I can't wait to have a girls' day out with you!"

She went on for a moment before Lyric was able to simply say, "Hi."

"So I need your help," Shanelle said, turning her attention back to me. "And if you want my forgiveness, you have to do me this solid."

I immediately felt uneasy. "What?"

Her smile was devilish. "Come with me."

I knew I wasn't going to like it.

As I stood on the stage with eleven other doms and looked over the crowd, my stomach churned slightly. I watched as each participant was auctioned off for a date night with the highest bidder with donations for my friend's group homes. Even though I tried to remind myself it was for a good cause, I felt like I was waiting to be sentenced.

I zoned out while the others were being auctioned off but immediately snapped out of it when I heard Shanelle say, "Ladies, I am especially excited about this next date. She is a part of my family. Ladies, meet Jazz Richardson!

"She has a degree in Psychology," she continued, "and she's an award-winning barber. What's better than having someone you can talk to who can keep that kitchen back there nice and lined up? And she's ready to show one of you ladies a great evening."

"Yay!"

I couldn't help but to smile when I heard Lyric yell from where she sat.

"It looks like you already have a fan," Shanelle said, her tone dripping with humor. Then, she stuck the microphone in front of my face, waiting for me to say something.

"Yeah, I guess," I told her and the audience. "My daughter, Lyric."

She stood up at the table, giving a little wave and curtsy to the people before sitting back down. Lyric was such a ham, but going by the looks of the bidders as they gazed at her, I think she made my property value go up.

"We will start the bidding at fifty dollars."

The first bid was immediately answered, followed by seventy-five dollars, then a hundred. To my surprise, the bidding had gotten up to five hundred dollars. Feeling myself, I started playing it up to the crowd.

Then, she shut it down.

"One thousand dollars."

I knew the voice instantly.

I looked over at JB and saw the expression on her face. It confirmed my suspicion.

Jordan Davis.

Where the hell did she come from?

I looked into the crowd and found her front and center amongst the group of bidders.

How the hell did I miss her?

"A thousand dollars!" Shanelle shouted in amazement into the microphone. "Is anybody ready to top that?"

They were murmurs in the crowd, and I silently prayed someone would speak up.

"Going once…"

Somebody, please.

"Going twice..."

Anybody. Please.

"Sold! For an amazing one thousand dollars!"

The audience clapped as Shanelle spoke again. "Jazz, go and meet your winning bidder!"

I tried to keep my game face on, but my feet felt like lead as I walked off the stage and down the steps to the side. I looked over at JB, who was shaking her head at me. I pointed at Lyric, and she nodded in understanding.

I took a breath before coming face to face with the woman who'd broken my heart.

"Long time, no see," she said casually.

"Yep," I replied, not really knowing what to say.

She was still fine as hell. From the looks of it, the years had been good to her. She was dressed in a dress so tight it looked painted on. I wondered how she was even able to stand on the stiletto heels she was wearing.

Her face was flawless. I had to force myself not to look at her lips. For a split moment, I remembered how they felt.

I didn't want to do this.

I didn't want to be anywhere near her.

"So how have you been?" she asked.

Her gaze felt like an invasion of my privacy as she gave me the once-over.

"I've been makin' it," I replied as nonchalantly as I could.

"You're looking good," she commented with a smile. "It looks like you've been doing pretty well for yourself. Award-winning barber, huh? I think I remember seeing you at one of the Bonner Brother events last year."

She began to walk, so I fell into step with her.

"Yeah," I replied. "I did Bonner Brothers last year. What were you doing there?"

"I participated, too," she answered.

"So you went ahead and made doing hair legal, huh?" I said as we made our way to one of the bars. "I thought you wanted to be a teacher or something."

"I am," she answered. "I do a little bit of teaching. I also have a few DVDs on extensions and wig making."

"Oh, so you're deep into doing the hair thing?" I said.

I hated to admit it, but I was kind of impressed.

She chuckled. "Yes. I love it. I travel all over doing what I love."

"Nothing wrong with that," I told her. "I guess you are doing alright for yourself since you're paying for thousand-dollar dates."

She chuckled again before turning to the bartender and ordering an apple Ciroc and Sprite.

"When I saw you, I was determined to win that bid. Drink?"

"No, thank you. I'm driving with my daughter in the car," I answered. "And why were you so determined to win the bid? We haven't spoken in years."

"I wanted to win *because* we haven't spoken in years," she answered. "And what's up with you having a daughter? I never knew about a daughter."

"She was before you," I answered, shrugging before continuing. "I guess we never got a chance to get close enough for me to share her with you. You made sure of that."

"Do you think it's possible for that situation to be rectified?" she wanted to know, her expression solemn.

"I don't really see how," I replied. "There's nothing to rectify. I've made peace with myself over that whole affair."

"Well, you still owe me a date," she responded with a

smirk. "Maybe we could at least talk. I find it interesting how we ended up taking similar paths."

"Similar paths? My path has led me to my daughter, and your path led you to a man. But, I guess we'll just have to see," I told her, taking a step back. "For now, I need to get back to my daughter."

Walking away from her like I was completely unaffected was the biggest challenge of the damn evening. I'd be lying if I said the encounter with her didn't leave me a little shaken.

As I walked back to the table, I let myself remember for a moment how crazy I had been about her and how sick I had been after she made me feel like a fool. Thankfully, the thoughts disappeared when I approached the table and found Melody sitting there.

I felt my smile spread across my lips.

"Well, hey there, Miss Superstar!"

The brown skin at her cheeks deepened. She looked down, almost shyly.

"Stop," she said with a bashful smile. "I'm not all that."

"Yes, you are," Lyric jumped in. "You are awesome!"

"Yes, she is," I agreed as I took my seat and looked directly at Melody.

"I definitely agree with that," Shanelle said enthusiastically while sitting next to JB. "Girl, you've got some serious pipes on you!"

"You should be on tour doing concerts and stuff," I told her. "You're a star in the making."

"Speaking of being a star," she said with a smile. "Look at you with your thousand-dollar bid. One of the highest bids of the night! Somebody wanted you bad!"

"Unfortunately," I replied, unable to keep from rolling my eyes.

"Sounds like there's a story behind that," she said.

I could read the interest in her eyes.

"Oh, there is," JB interjected willingly.

"We'll have to talk about that some other time," I replied, looking at Melody.

"Do you know her?" Lyric asked.

"I used to," I answered, being as honest as I could.

I saw Melody's eyebrow raise in curiosity.

"Another time," I told her. Changing the subject, I turned to Shanelle and asked, "Just how did you get this lovely songbird on your roster?"

"Would you believe me if I told you karaoke?" she replied. "I saw her at one of the karaoke spots I go to. So, I just asked if she wanted to make a little money. At first, she looked at me crazy, but when I explained, she was down for it."

"I couldn't resist doing something to help out the community," Melody chimed in.

"And I appreciate it so much," Shanelle said with a grin. "Now, my question is how do the two of you know each other?"

"We live next door to each other," I answered quickly.

"So you guys are just neighbors?"

I already knew what Shanelle was trying to get at.

"We're just friends," I cleared up.

"Oh, okay," she said.

I saw the look she exchanged with JB and shook my head to myself in amusement. I then looked over at Melody and found her watching me. I'm not sure what it was exactly, but the look in her eyes had my mental dick standing at attention. It was so intense that I had to excuse myself from the table.

I took a minute to compose myself in the bathroom.

This is Melody, I told myself. *We have a good friendship growing.*

Don't fuck that up.

However, even as I told myself these things, I pictured her up on that stage singing, looking sexy as ever…looking at me…singing to *me*. I thought about how she smiled and how her hips swayed when she walked. Then I imagined how she would sound once I dipped my head between her thighs and made her sing a completely different tune.

In that moment, it hit me just how bad I wanted her.

I had to shake that shit off and do it fast.

But how?

FIGHTING THE FEELING

"You look nice tonight."

"So do you. I admit I was surprised that you had come back to me so fast. You were a little icy when you walked away."

"I apologize for that. Let's grow from me coming back to ask you out."

It had been a week since the fundraiser, and I now found myself looking across the table at my ex. Even though I would've been lying if I said she wasn't looking as edible as a five-course meal, I knew the only reason I'd gone ahead and asked her out was because my attraction to Melody bugged me. I mean, I could handle Melody being pretty, or hell, even fine. But, I wasn't ready for how my whole fucking being reacted to her the night of the fundraiser.

She was my neighbor. We were growing closer in this friendship thing, and I kind of liked it. I didn't want the messiness that could come with breaking her off. And though I wouldn't admit it to anyone, the thought of getting involved with someone emotionally scared me a little. I wasn't ready for that. The only emotional entanglement I wanted was with my daughter.

So, there I sat, looking at Jordan as she talked to me as if she hadn't stomped on my heart years before.

"The fundraiser was a lovely event," she was saying as we waited for our first course of dinner.

"It was," I agreed. "I'm proud of how my friends put it together. They raised a lot of money, too. Almost thirty thousand, I think."

"I was very impressed," she replied. "I might have to look into it and see what I can do to help. Maybe make a donation to the cause."

"I'm sure they would appreciate that," I responded. "I plan to donate a few manhours to help get it together. Maybe even do a little mentoring. I thought about offering my services to help them get groomed up for job interviews and whatnot."

"That's very commendable," Jordan replied. "I might consider offering a service or two like that. I like that idea. Maybe we can work on something together to offer the kids."

I took a swig of my drink, refusing to give a response committing to that. Instead, I changed the subject.

"Speaking of services, I see you finally decided to take on hairstyling as a career. What brought that on?"

"Yes," she said, sitting up straighter. I could tell she was proud of herself. "Well, my mom and my sis still do hair. When we were in school, it was just a hustle to me, though. I always thought I was going to be a teacher, but once I finished school, I ended up getting a desk job instead. I got bored sitting at a desk real fast. I still had folks who were asking me to split their wigs in my free time, and it just hit me, ya know. *I actually love doing this.* Fast forward a few years and here I am, getting paid to do what I love and getting ready to open my second shop in Stone Mountain."

"Well, I'm glad you are doing so well for yourself," I told her as our waiter brought our salads.

"Thank you," she said, smiling proudly. "And what about you? What made you decide to become a barber? If I remember correctly, you wanted to focus on psychology."

"Truthfully..." I began, taking a quick forkful of my salad into my mouth to gauge whether there was enough dressing on it. I chewed for a moment and nodded to myself as I swallowed. "...trying to get over you is what led me down this path."

"Awww, come on-"

"No, seriously," I continued, interrupting her before she could finish. "I don't think you understand how hurt I was behind all of that shit. Don't worry, though. I've moved on since then. But, at the time, I wanted to erase anything that reminded me of you. That included my hair. I thought about how much you loved my hair, so I went to the barbershop and had it all chopped off."

She gasped in surprise. "Are you for real? You did that because of me?"

"I'm as serious as a heart attack," I informed her. "After I looked at the hair on the floor and then took in my reflection, I loved it. I actually felt an immediate sense of freedom with the cut. And I have to say, I thought I looked pretty damn good. I liked how I felt afterwards, and I liked the environment in the barbershop. It's like something just clicked in me. I knew right then that it was something I wanted to do. I still got my degree, though. I worked too hard to give that up, but I immediately went on to get my barbering license and haven't looked back since. One of these days, I might get like you and open up my own spot, but for now, I'm more focused on my relationship with my daughter."

"Tell me about her," Jordan requested.

I saw her eyes light up with interest, and for a second, I debated on whether I wanted to share that part of my life with her. After a moment, I decided it wouldn't hurt to share a little. Hell, I would brag to a stranger about my daughter. The least I could do was share a bite of information with my ex.

"What can I say about Lyric?" I began, unable to stop a smile from creeping across my face. "She's an amazing little girl. She's smart, talented, and plays the piano. She's pretty good at it, too. She impresses me, and I don't say that about very many people."

"How old is she?"

"Almost ten," I answered, taking a sip of my drink.

"Ten?" she replied. "Then she was around when we were in college."

"She was alive," I responded, "but she wasn't around. She was…in special care while I got myself together. I got pregnant with her young and had no idea what to do with a baby. A very special friend of mine took her in so I could get my life together. And now that I have, I have my baby girl."

It felt good to say that. My smile on the inside was bigger than the one on my face.

"Well, you look like every bit of the proud parent," she commented with a soft smile.

"I'm still getting the hang of being a parent," I replied. "But, yeah, I'm enjoying it, and I *am* proud."

"I like that," she said. "Well, maybe one day soon I will get to meet her."

Don't get too comfortable too fast, shorty, I thought to myself. Instead, I took a sip of my wine and gave her a casual, "Maybe."

"Where is she now anyway?" Jordan asked.

"At a friend's," I answered.

"One of hers or one of yours?" she quizzed.

"One of *ours*," I clarified before leaning back in my seat to look her in the eyes. "Just ask, Jordan."

"Are you seeing someone?"

"If I was, I wouldn't be here."

"Oh," she replied, looking down at her salad for a second before looking back up at me.

I could clearly read the look in her eyes before she opened her mouth to speak.

"Ya know, we can get this to-go and find a more intimate setting."

Even as I told myself it was a bad idea, I got our waiter's attention to have him bag up the rest of our meal.

I don't remember getting the food out of the car. I don't remember the drive to my house. I don't even remember unlocking the front door.

But, none of that mattered as she pushed me against the wall as soon as we were inside. She was as aggressive as I remembered, taking my mouth with hers. But, I wasn't the same person she knew in college, and I quickly took control of the situation.

I turned her around and pressed her back up against the wall, never pulling my mouth away from hers. I felt her intake of breath as my hand went under her skirt. Her skin was warm and smooth against my fingertips. I wanted to know what else was warm. My hands moved from her thighs and cupped her ass cheeks only to find she wasn't wearing any panties.

"You came prepared, huh?" I asked against her lips.

"I can't say I wasn't a little hopeful," she admitted,

moaning as I kissed her neck.

"Mmmhmm," I said against her skin. "Let's take this to the bedroom."

Happy to comply, she took my hand and led the way as if she had already been to my bedroom before. I was amused by it, smiling a bit as we entered my bedroom.

I grabbed the remote to my stereo, turned it on, and turned it up. A slow groove streamed from the satellite radio.

I escorted Jordan to the bed and laid her down on it. Then, I kneeled over her and lowered my upper body take her lips back with mine. Again, I slid my hand under her skirt, this time slipping my fingers between the moist lips at her center. She moaned against my mouth and immediately arched her back in response.

I knew she was ready.

I toyed with her, massaging her clitoris for a minute before sliding two fingers inside of her. Her hips jerked in response. She grabbed my hand, trying to push my fingers in deeper. She thrusted her pelvis upward urgently.

I remembered exactly how she liked it when we were younger. It seemed it hadn't changed. I mentally prepared myself to give her what she wanted.

And then I was ruined.

The sound of the music filled my ears before Jill Scott's voice came through the speaker. The tune "Come See Me" caressed my ear canal, and then all I could see was her.

Melody.

My mind immediately went back to when she was on stage, singing that very song while looking at me. My fingers hesitated in their manipulation of Jordan's flesh, and the taste of her lips immediately became subpar.

What the fuck?

Even as I slowly pulled away from her, the devil on my shoulder screamed in my ear, *What the fuck are you doing?*

Jordan looked up at me with confusion on her face as I removed my hand and backed away.

"Is everything okay?" she asked, concern etched on her face.

"Yeah," I lied. "Sorry. I just need to go to the bathroom."

"Oh," she replied. "Well, I'll be waiting for you right here."

"Okay," I said before turning on my heels and making my way to my bathroom.

I closed the door behind me and locked it as if I could block out both her and the sound of the music. Jill Scott's lyrics taunted me, ushering in visions of Melody that I couldn't seem to wipe away.

In my bedroom, on my bed, was a woman that I'd been in love with, who I had craved for a long time after she'd left me. She was ready and wide open to receive me.

But, I didn't want her.

I admitted to myself that, other than trying to get past my attraction to my friend, another one of the reasons she was even there was so I could prove to myself that I could still have her and walk away afterwards.

But, I no longer even wanted to do that.

I looked in the mirror and shook my head at myself.

I'd had more than my fair share of women, easily sexing them and sending them on their way with the understanding that it was all in fun and I was in no way looking for a commitment. Now I stood in my bathroom feeling like I was about to cheat on a woman who wasn't even mine. I laughed a little as I turned on the faucet to wash my hands.

I can't do this shit. There's no point in even trying.

After scrubbing my hands with citrus-scented soap to remove Jordan's essence and scent from my skin, I dried my hands and opened the bathroom door. As I walked into my bedroom, Jordan was re-entering the room from the front.

"Is everything okay?" she asked, walking over to me.

She attempted to wrap her arms around my neck, but I stopped her, gently taking her hands and putting them down at her sides.

"Baby, what's wrong?" she wanted to know.

"Nothing's wrong," I answered. "I just can't do this."

I released her hands and went to turn off my stereo.

"What's the problem?" she questioned. After a pause, she asked, "Is there somebody else?"

I hesitated to answer, but finally spoke. "Something like that."

"Is it the girl from the fundraiser?" she asked. "The singer?"

How on earth did she come to that conclusion?

I asked her as much, and she hesitated for a moment before answering.

"I remember seeing you talking to her. Is it her?"

For a moment, I was quiet. That was enough of an answer for her.

She smoothed her hair down in the back and adjusted her clothing. "Take me home, Jazz."

I had absolutely no problem with that.

It was a quiet drive to her house. After telling her goodnight, I watched her walk stiffly to her front door. I didn't pull off until I saw her go inside.

She was pissed, but that wasn't my problem.

As I headed back to my house, I checked my phone. I had a message from the woman who had somehow managed to become the apple of my eye.

Lyric isn't feeling too great. She can just stay here tonight. She's already asleep.

After stopping at a red light, I texted back, *Are you sure it's not a problem?*

A few moments later, she responded, *It's fine.*

As the light turned green, I sent back a quick *Thank you,* then rerouted my destination.

I didn't want the uneaten food from my failed date. I opted for a waffle, eggs, and sausage from the nearest Waffle House. After getting a seat and placing my order, I checked my phone and saw the last message from Melody.

That's what friends are for!

I shook my head as I waited for my coffee.

Friend.

I no longer wanted her to be just my friend.

For the first time in years, I wanted someone to be mine.

I wanted *her* to be mine.

Fuck.

REVELATIONS

"Hey, Ma. Is it okay if I go over to Mel's house? She's going to teach me a new song today."

I looked up from playing my video game to respond to my daughter.

"I guess so. When are you going over there?"

"In a few minutes, if that's okay," she replied. "I just have to put my shoes on and grab a snack for us."

"Oh, so you're sneaking snacks over there to her, huh?" I joked.

She laughed before answering. "I don't want to be selfish and take just one oatmeal cream pie. Nana always told me to be thoughtful."

"Well, that's nice of you," I told her. "You can go for a little while, but not too long. We're going out to eat tonight since I don't feel like cooking."

"Okay," Lyric replied before running back into her room to get ready to go spend some time with Melody. "Thank you!" she yelled from her room.

"You're welcome!" I called back.

A couple minutes later, I stood on my front porch and watched her make her way over to the house next door. I watched as Melody came out onto her front porch and greeted Lyric with a hug. She glanced in my direction and gave me a quick wave before escorting her little friend into the house.

I hadn't seen her much since the night I went out with Jordan. She had come by a couple of times, but I'd gotten used to seeing her almost every day. So, only seeing her those couple of times felt odd to me. And even then, she and Lyric would end up going over to her place.

It hit me that in the short time we'd known each other, I had never been inside her house.

That shit bothered me.

I sat on the couch playing my game and asking myself why she had never invited me over, and I couldn't come up with a reason. Maybe it wasn't her. Maybe it was me. I mean, she had become so comfortable coming to my house that I had gotten comfortable with it, too. It never even occurred to me to do the neighbor thing and go visit her.

Maybe that's why she stopped coming by so much, I thought to myself. *Maybe she feels like she's putting in most of the effort in this friendship we're building.*

I felt the need to remedy that.

I turned off my game system and got up to go in the kitchen. After going through my cabinets and grabbing a few items, I decided I would go ahead and make dinner. Within an hour, I had whipped up some spaghetti, a tossed salad, and some garlic bread. After putting everything in containers, I packed them in a couple of grocery bags and headed over to the house next door.

I could hear them laughing and tinkering at Melody's piano keys as I stepped on her porch. Her front door was open, so I was able to watch them for a moment through the glass of her screen door. My daughter looked like she was having the time of her life as Melody jokingly played a Little

Richard tune.

I took a peek at the surrounding area while I was still somewhat incognito. I took in the hardwood floors and warm tones of her living room. The mahogany hue and the designs on her piano made me think it had been custom made. It fit right in with the warm browns and deep reds of her living room furniture and the area rug that her coffee table sat on. There were various paintings on the walls as well as a few portraits and one huge frame filled with various snapshots. I wanted to get closer to have a better look at what I thought might be a little of her history.

It looked comfortable.

It looked like a place where love existed.

I hoped in time my own place would be similar.

Shaking the thoughts from my mind, I refocused on the task at hand. I reached out and pressed the doorbell.

They both looked up and at me.

Lyric's smile grew bigger. Melody's faltered a bit.

It immediately struck me as odd. But, I tried to brush it off as she got up and came to the door.

"What are you doing here?" she asked, opening the screen door.

She stepped aside, and I stepped over the threshold.

I held up the bags. "I made dinner."

She shook her head slightly. "You really didn't have to do that," she said, sounding a little hesitant.

"Well, you do it for us all the time," I replied, walking further into her home. "So, let's just call this me paying you back a little bit. Where's the kitchen?"

She seemed even more hesitant, but she quickly masked it before leading me towards her kitchen. Something felt awkward and I didn't like it, but I pushed on as if I hadn't noticed.

"You have a nice house," I told her as I placed the bags down on one of the kitchen counters.

I looked around. Her kitchen made mine look like a closet.

"Thank you," she replied. The smile on her face then was genuine. "My granddaddy left it for me in his will. They lived here for years before buying something a little smaller. When I was growing up, we'd have our family get-togethers and dinners here on Sundays."

Her eyes took on a far away look as she continued.

"When he got sick, he and my gran moved into my parents' house. My mom didn't want my gran to have to go through everything on her own. I was living in the dorm at school, but he told me that the house would be mine as long as I promised to take care of it. He passed away when I was twenty. I moved out of my dorm and into this house, and I've been here ever since."

For a moment, we were both quiet. I appreciated her sharing a piece of herself with me.

When she cleared her throat, I knew she was about to change the subject.

"I didn't mean to bore you with that history lesson," she said suddenly. "What's for dinner?"

"It wasn't boring at all," I told her. "Thank you for sharing it with me."

Her cheeks reddened and she looked away, almost shyly.

I felt a flutter in my stomach. Before I allowed myself to put too much thought into it, I refocused on the task at hand. I opened the first bag and started removing items.

"My world-famous spaghetti, a tossed salad, and some garlic bread," I announced.

"I thought we were going out to eat," Lyric chimed in as

she came into the kitchen.

"I changed my mind," I answered with a shrug.

"That's cool," my daughter replied. "I like your spaghetti anyway."

"Well, go wash your hands in the bathroom," Melody instructed her. "I'll help Jazz get our plates together."

"Yes, ma'am," Lyric said with a small smile before leaving the kitchen.

She was already so familiar with our neighbor's place, and there I was seeing it for the first time.

Melody and I moved towards the sink at the same time. We nearly bumped into each other, but she swerved out of the way just in time.

"You can go first," she said, stepping back.

"There's room for both of us," I told her, inching aside so we could wash our hands before plating up the food. "I promise I won't bite."

She walked back to the sink slowly and turned on the faucet. After giving the water time to get hot, we both stood there washing our hands quietly. We usually had light exchanges, but the silence was almost deafening.

I looked at her. "Are we okay?" I asked suddenly.

"What do you mean?" she asked, while tearing a couple of paper towel sheets off a nearby roll.

"Something's different," I said, accepting the paper towels she handed to me. "Did I do something wrong?"

"What do you mean?" she asked, glancing my way briefly before opening a cabinet and pulling out a few plates.

"You haven't been coming over as much," I began. "Not to mention, you seem kinda distant."

"I've just been trying to give you guys a little space," she replied. "I don't want to become a pain-"

"No," I interrupted. "You see Lyric just as much as you always have. You just bring her over here instead. So what is it for real? What did I do for you to not want to be around me anymore? On some real shit, I actually thought we kinda made a connection at the fundraiser."

"Yeah," she said with a small nod. "So did I."

For a moment, we stood there wordless. I wanted to say something but wasn't quite sure what it was that I wanted to say yet. My daughter kept me from having to think too hard on it.

"Is the food ready?"

We both looked at her as she came back into the kitchen.

"Almost, kid," I told her.

"Can you grab us a few drinks out of the fridge?" Melody asked her. "We'll have food on the table in just a minute."

I watched her for a second as she grabbed the bowl of spaghetti.

"Can you grab the salad and bread?" she asked in a tone that was as sweet as Splenda.

"Sure," I replied, doing as requested. "I'm not through talking about this, though," I warned her.

"I am," she threw back, then walked out of the kitchen.

There was definitely something fishy in the water, and I wanted to know what.

We made it through the dinner, courtesy of Lyric coming up with a ton of things to talk about, including her upcoming school year. By the time we finished eating, she had convinced Melody to come with us to the upcoming orientation.

Later that evening, I lay on my couch remembering how she smiled when Lyric finally convinced her to say yes. Then,

I remembered how she looked at me afterwards. The smile stayed in place, but her eyes had changed. The sparkle wasn't there.

What the fuck did I do?

I needed to know.

I got up from the couch and went to check on Lyric. After making sure she was asleep, I checked the time on my watch.

9:45.

I was sure she was still awake. So, I threw on a pair of Nikes and grabbed my keys. I crept out of the house, locking the door behind me. After crossing the distance that separated Melody's house from mine and making my way to her front door, I rang the doorbell and waited for her to answer. I felt a quick flutter in my stomach as I heard her unlocking the door.

When she opened it, she just stood there looking at me through the screen door.

Melody was wearing a purple cotton robe and a pair of matching furry slippers. Her face was free of the little makeup she had on earlier, and in spite of the uncomfortable look on her face, she looked absolutely beautiful.

"Bad time?" I inquired.

"I was just about to lay down," she answered.

"Can we talk?" I asked her through the door.

"What is there to talk about?" Melody questioned, pushing her hands into the pockets of her robe.

"That's what I'm trying to figure out," I answered.

When she didn't respond, I looked around before looking back at her.

"Are you going to make me stand out here to talk to you? These mosquitos are fuckin' me up."

After a slight hesitation, she unlocked the screen door and

stepped to the side to allow me inside her home for the second time that day.

"I won't hold you up for long," I promised her. "I don't want to leave Lyric by herself at the house for too long, but I have to know what's going on."

"Why does something have to be going on?" she asked as she closed the front door and leaned against it.

"Because you barely even look in my direction now," I began. "And when you do, it's like you refuse to make eye contact with me. I just want to know what I did to you. I thought we were working on this friendship thing, and now I kinda feel like I'm losing you."

I cringed on the inside. I hadn't meant to say it quite like that, but hell, it was already out there now.

She stood there for a minute before saying anything. I stood there waiting and watching her. Finally, she spoke but without looking at me.

"I just figured it would be a good idea to give you a little space."

"But why?" I wanted to know. "Did I ever say anything to you about needing some space?"

"You didn't have to," she snapped. "Your girlfriend answering the door was enough for me."

"My girlfriend?" I repeated, completely confused. "What girlfriend? What on earth are you talking about?"

"The night you went out and asked me to keep Lyric for you," she began.

I felt a touch of anxiety as she continued.

"Remember, Lyric wasn't feeling too good? When I saw your car at home so soon after you left, I figured your date was over. I brought Lyric home so she could sleep comfortably in her own bed."

I felt a weight in my stomach that was as heavy as a boulder.

"We used the spare key and walked right in," she continued. "And there she stood. It was obvious we had interrupted something. She said you were in the bathroom. I apologized for the intrusion, and she hinted at the possibility of you two being busy for a while. Then, she winked at me on top of that. So, I just took Lyric back home with me. Not too long after that, I looked outside and your car was gone. I figured the two of you were working things out, so I didn't want to be in the way."

For a minute, all I could do was look at her. She almost looked sad. In that moment, I knew she was vulnerable, and that affected me in a way I hadn't been prepared for. I wanted to reassure her. I wanted to soothe her. I wanted to reach out and touch her.

But, I didn't.

As a matter of fact, I shoved my hands into my pockets just to keep from reaching out to her. I shook my head.

"Nothing happened, Mel."

"I'm not a child, Jazz," she responded. "And I'm not stupid. I know what getting run up and done up looks like. And your girlfriend looked like-"

"She's not my girlfriend," I corrected. "And, yes, we were about to fuck, but I couldn't do it."

"Why not?" she wanted to know.

Because she wasn't you was the response that popped into my head, but I refused to share that. So, instead, I countered with, "Why does it matter?"

She looked away. "It doesn't."

As hard as I was trying, I couldn't resist anymore. I took my hand out of my pocket and turned her face so I could see her eyes.

"It mattered enough for you to not want to be around me," I told her. "Why?"

She was quiet for a second, but then looked me in the eyes when she answered my question.

"Because I thought *we* had made some kind of connection."

"I thought so, too," I confessed.

"If that's the case, why did you go out with her? Why were you so ready to have sex with her? Why not me?"

I wasn't expecting that. I guess my face gave that away.

"I mean," she began quickly, "if we both felt this connection, why haven't you pursued me at all? Why did you go out with her?"

"Honestly," I began, shaking my head at myself, "I was being lazy."

Seeing her confused expression, I continued. "I know her. She's familiar. She's easy; however, my feelings for her are no longer what they used to be. But, *you*…" I shook my head again and smiled. "You are new. I'm still trying to figure you out. You're going to require work… and you kinda scare me."

"Scare you?" She laughed. "*I* scare *you*? The female version of Leon Phelps?"

I had to laugh with her at that one. "Where the hell did you get that from? *The Ladies Man*? Really?"

"Well, maybe Bill Bellamy in *How to Be a Player*," she continued, rolling her eyes upward as if she were in deep thought.

"I'm really not that bad," I told her. "Where are you getting your information from?"

"I refuse to reveal my source," she answered jokingly.

"It was Shanelle, wasn't it?" I asked, already figuring out the answer.

When I saw her lip twitch, my answer was confirmed. I laughed.

"You can't go by what Shanelle says about me. She exaggerates."

"So you didn't always hit on her best friend?"

"That was for fun," I replied, still laughing. "So you've been checking up on me, huh?"

She chuckled. "I won't say all that," Melody answered. "She actually asked me about us the night of the fundraiser."

"Oh really?" I asked, my interest at an all-time high. "So what did you ladies discuss?"

"Well," she began, clearing her throat, "she told me that you had a way with the ladies, but you're a good person. I told her that I believed her."

"Okay, I can accept that," I said with a nod. "What else?"

"She also told me that you aren't big on relationships, so be careful."

"Careful?" I repeated.

I didn't like how it sounded, but I couldn't argue that summary either.

"Anything else?"

"Yeah," she replied with a shy smile, then grew quiet.

"Well?" I wanted to know.

"She told me that she'd never seen you look at someone the way you looked at me."

It was my turn to look away for a second. *Shanelle talks way too damn much.*

"Was she telling truth?" Melody asked. "Or was she exaggerating?"

I looked back at her then. We'd gotten all of that out, so

why stop there?

"She was telling the truth," I answered quietly.

"And how do you look at me?" she asked bashfully.

I took a deep breath before slowly answering, "Like I've never seen a perfect creation before."

Hearing her quick intake of breath, I decided to continue.

"I've never met someone who is so giving and caring. I didn't know women like you existed, at least not for me. And you're a fuckin' goddess; yet, you're humble. The only thing more mind-blowing than the curves of your body is the curve of your lips when you smile at me. I've wanted to kiss you since the first time I saw you."

I didn't realize I had pressed myself against her until I felt her hand on my shoulder.

"So what's stopping you now?" she challenged.

Her tone was breathless and made it harder for me to remain in a platonic friend's place. I was trying, but so many truths were coming out.

"I don't want to fuck up what we already have just because I want to kiss you," I answered.

"The only thing you will fuck up," she began, "is this moment if you don't kiss me right now."

She didn't have to tell me but once.

I threw caution to the wind, said a silent prayer that I wasn't making a mistake, and moved in on her barely-glossed lips. I wasn't sure what I expected, but it wasn't this. I admit I'd imagined it once or twice, but it was never quite like this.

I never really cared for lemons, but the taste of strawberry lemonade was fresh on her tongue and as intoxicating as liquor. It fed my entire fucking soul. In that moment, I was dying of thirst, and she replenished me.

As I pulled her closer to me, her tongue slid across mine

as though we had kissed millions of times in our past lives. I had expected her to be shy, maybe even a little hesitant with this being our first kiss, but she was far from it.

It wasn't like she was aggressive or anything like that. She was simply confident, and I could feel it in the way she held on to me as her arms overlapped against the back of my neck. It was like she knew all along that we were supposed to at least have this moment, and she had been waiting on my ass to get with the program and figure it out.

Everything about her kiss felt…right.

And it threw me for a fucking loop.

I wanted to run. Whether it was away from her or deeper into her, I wasn't sure.

I felt lightheaded. I felt butterflies in my stomach and shit. It felt like my heart was about to beat a hole into my chest to free itself as I finally made myself pull away from her.

Her eyes sparkled as she looked at me.

Lord, the way she was looking at me made me ache to reach inside that damn robe to explore the skin beneath it.

But, it was too soon.

Too. Fucking. Soon.

"You know," she began as she gently wiped away a bit of her lip gloss from the corner of my mouth, "we don't have to stay right here at the door."

I could hear the desire in her voice, and it took every ounce of my willpower to remain cool. I had to clear my throat before I could even speak.

"It's probably best if we stay right here."

After the way she had just made love to my mouth, she had the audacity to look embarrassed.

"I-"

"Before you say anything," I interrupted her, placing my

index finger on her lips, "the only reason I'm saying this is because my daughter is home asleep right now. I can't just leave her over there like that."

Her expression changed to one of understanding and then relief.

"I understand," she said softly.

"And," I continued, "I don't want to rush this. With the way I'm feeling right now, if we even stepped in your front room, we wouldn't make it to your bedroom."

She had the nerve to blush.

Damn, she's beautiful.

I needed to get the fuck out of there.

We'd made enough discoveries for one night. If I stayed there much longer, I would know her in the biblical sense before the night was over.

"I need to get back over to the house before Lyric wakes up and wonders where I am," I told her.

"Okay," she said with a nod. "Give her a kiss on the forehead for me."

"I can do that," I told her, wrapping my arms around her waist one more time. "Can I get one, too?"

"Not on your forehead," she replied, before meeting me halfway for another kiss.

I swear my toes damn near curled from the sensation of kissing her. I shook my head a little when I finally came up for air. I reached behind her to open the door so I could step out. I waited for her to lock her screen door before speaking.

"Goodnight, Mel," I almost whispered.

"Goodnight, Leon Phelps," she giggled.

"Oh, you got jokes," I said with a laugh.

"A few," she replied, flashing those pearly whites. Her tone changed after she stared at me for a second. "See you tomorrow?"

It was a question more than a statement.

"Hell, yeah," I answered, staring into her eyes through the glass panel.

"Well then, goodnight, Jazz."

"Goodnight," I said again.

I watched her close the door before I descended the steps and made my way back to my house. I was as geeked as a teenaged girl who just experienced her first kiss. Hell, I even wanted to call my best friend and tell her about the shit.

But, I maintained.

I checked on Lyric before going to take a shower. Afterwards, I lay in my bed replaying what had happened. I could still feel her lips against mine. The taste of her tongue was burned into my memory, and I feared it would haunt me for the rest of my damn life.

I fell asleep excited about the days to come.

Excited and scared as fuck.

TAKING IT SLOW

I left work early. My mind had been full of what had occurred the night before, and I needed a little *me* time before picking Lyric up from the center. I found myself sitting at a table in Southlake Mall chatting it up with my confidant.

"So what's the issue?"

I looked at JB and laughed. "Why does there have to be an issue?"

"Because I know you," she answered. "You don't just call out of the blue offering to take me to lunch and shit. At least not since I've been married."

"You know I try not to interfere with your married life," I told her.

"You know married folks do have lives outside of each other, right?" she threw back. "But, fuck all that. What's going on with you?"

Sparing no details, I told her about the night with Jordan and what happened with Melody.

"So what are you going to do?" she wanted to know.

"I don't know," I answered, taking a swig of my soda. "I know I'm completely through with Jordan's ass, though."

"Are you sure about that?"

"Hell yeah," I answered. "I couldn't even fuck her because my mind went to Melody. Shit's fuckin' crazy!"

"Maybe you're feeling more for her than you are ready to admit," JB replied. "From what you say, she seems more than ready to give you guys a try. So what are you scared of?"

"I'm not good at this relationship shit," I confessed. "It just doesn't work for me."

"How do you know?" my best friend challenged. "You've only done it once since I've known you. And before you try to argue, fuckin' a girl for three weeks straight is not a relationship."

I laughed at my friend and shook my head. "I know that!"

"You wanna know what I think it is," she asked, leaning in like she was about to share the secret of life with me.

I looked at her, waiting.

"I think you feel way more for her than you have for anyone in a while, and that shit scares you."

"Why do you keep saying that shit?" I asked, trying to sound nonchalant.

"Because I know that feeling," she answered, wiping her fingertips on a napkin. "You've met my wife, right? Sometimes shit happens when you least expect it. I think you should let it. It might be good for you."

"That's easy for you to say," I told my friend. "You got the girl."

"Do you remember what I went through to get her, though?" she retorted. "And hell, you're older than me. You can't be a player forever. You ain't tired of shuffling these broads around yet? You don't think this girl might at least be worth a try? Stop being so afraid, bitch. Go for it."

So, there I stood looking at my reflection in the mirror, trying to make sure I hadn't overdressed for the day's events.

I'd been on tons of dates and had even been out with her

before, but Lyric was always with us. This was different. This time, it was just the two of us. Working towards…something.

I had gotten accustomed to dinners, movies, and then fucking. Sometimes both dinner and the movie were skipped. Some nights, I'd end up at my date's house; sometimes, they ended up at mine, with an Uber or Lyft request to transport them home later that night. We always knew what we were getting together for.

But, this was something else. The endgame was a mystery. The goal of the entire day was to just enjoy each other's company and get to know each other better. Even though I was a little nervous, that's exactly what I planned to do.

I looked in the mirror, checking to make sure my freshly done haircut was on point. After rolling on a bit of the body oil I had made just for me, I grabbed my keys and headed for the door.

I took deep breaths as I locked my door and walked the distance that separated Melody's house from mine. As usual, she had her front door open and her screen door secured. I stood at the door listening as she playfully belted out the song playing on her radio.

Lord, her voice stirred something in me. It still amazed me how that beautiful voice came from her. It hypnotized me, and everything around me almost seemed to vanish.

She looked up and saw me standing at the door. A beautiful smile grew across her face, and it took my breath away for a moment. She walked over and opened the door.

"Hi," she said, beaming.

"Hey," I said back, taking in her appearance.

The multi-colored sundress hugged her top half and flared from her waist down. The material fell against her full hips, and for a second, I was jealous of the clothing. Her wedged sandals gave her almost three more inches of height and showcased a pair of pretty feet with toenails that bore fuchsia-colored polish.

"You're so fuckin' pretty," I told her and smiled when I saw the color deepen on her cheeks.

"Thank you," she replied, almost shyly. "You look nice yourself."

I glanced down at the tan cargo shorts, blue short-sleeve button-up, and matching Sperry shoes that I wore.

"I dunno," I replied. "You make me wanna go home and change."

"You look perfect, I promise," she told me, and I think I felt my own face get a little warm.

"Are you ready?" I asked, taking the attention off of myself.

"Yep," she answered. "I just need to grab my purse."

I watched her sashay towards the room I had yet to see. Her bedroom.

Just the thought of it woke my whole damn body up, but I mentally tried to calm myself down. *That's not what today is about. This is our first date, and we're taking it slow.*

But, damn! Seeing her in that sundress was fucking with my focus.

"Okay," she said, coming out of her bedroom. "I'm ready."

Me, too. You have no idea.

"Alright then," I replied, trying to shake the thoughts that were creeping into my head. "Let's ride."

It was a beautiful afternoon. Our first stop was Piedmont Park. We walked around, making small talk as we took in the sights of the diverse groups of people who also wanted to spend their afternoon in the park. Couples, straight and gay; families that consisted of parents and several children or parents and their pets; random musicians gracefully accepting the coins tossed their way or basking in the thrill of having an audience held captive as they performed a set. They were all there, live and in vivid color, enjoying the beauty of the afternoon.

It was a lovely sight to see.

However, nothing compared to the woman who was walking beside me. I tried to play it off, but I could hardly keep my eyes off of her. She laughed at my jokes and even called me corny when they missed the mark. We gossiped and created stories about the people who were walking around the park.

Melody was creative and had a twisted sense of humor, which I loved. She managed to make me laugh, and it wasn't just little chuckles. I mean, loud cackles. In spite of her looking like a goddess, she wasn't afraid to be silly in public and even danced amongst a group of folks who looked like gypsies or modern-day hippies or something. By the time they were done, she'd made new friends.

In that same moment, I accepted the fact that I was in love with her.

It hit me like a ton of bricks.

It wasn't just infatuation. It wasn't just desire. It sure as hell wasn't just liking her a lot.

It was love.

Butterflies-in-my-stomach, is-this-shit-real, my-heart-is-racing…love.

I could only stare at her as she walked back towards me.

How'd she do it? I asked myself in the back of my mind. *How did she get in?*

"You okay?" she asked, taking in my appearance. Her smile turned into a look of concern.

"I'm cool," I answered, struggling to put back on my air of being cool, calm, and collected. "Did you have fun twerking over there?"

Her smile returned and she laughed. "I was hardly twerking," she replied. "It was fun, though. You should join in next time."

"All of that spinning and shit?" I voiced with mock indignation. "I'll let you have that."

She easily linked her arm around mine, and we were off again.

Before long, we found ourselves at the botanical garden. After paying our admission, I escorted her through the stunning garden.

"So do you do this often?" I asked her as we walked along a cemented trail.

"Do what often?" Melody asked, while keeping in step with me.

"Go out with women," I answered.

"Not often," she replied. "I have a few times before, but it's been a while. I dated a girl for about six months back in college. I was terrified of what my folks would say when they found out. But, they thought it was a phase and figured I would grow out of it. My mother even sat down with me one day and said she thought it was normal to be a little curious. It made me wonder if she had been a little curious herself at one point."

We both chuckled at that.

"What's so special about me for you to break your hiatus from women?" I wanted to know.

"I wish I could give you a clear answer," she began, "but

there's so much. I've been drawn to you for a while. I dig your aura. You're funny. I can see the love you have for your daughter. It's a combination of everything I've learned about you. I want to learn so much more. The good, the bad, and the ugly."

"Are you sure this isn't just a curiosity thing you have for me?" I needed to know the answer to that question now more than I've ever wanted to before.

"Yes," she answered. "I'm positive it isn't just about being curious. We've kissed, and I don't think it's something I want to stop doing anytime soon."

I swear my clit jumped. But, I played it cool.

"Oh really?" I challenged as we stopped in front of the magnificent botanical sculpture known as the Earth Goddess. I stepped in front of her, facing her, and took both of her hands into mine. "How about right now?"

"What about right now?" she asked, looking up at me.

"Kiss me now," I dared her, then nodded my head towards the sculpture. "I don't think she's going to mind."

In my mind, I told myself that I was testing her. I figured she would never do it in a public place despite telling me that she wasn't new to being with a woman.

I felt my heart start to race when she pulled one of her hands from mine to gently touch my face. It was the softest touch I'd ever felt, and I thought I was going to melt from the sweetness of the simple caress. She eased onto her tiptoes. I met her halfway, brushing her lips with mine. The hand that had been touching my cheek found its way to the back of my neck as she pulled me into her.

The kiss was sweet, simple, and lingering.

As a cool breeze surrounded us on the warm day, it seemed as though our moment had been blessed by the Earth

Goddess herself.

It took a moment for us to pull apart, but when we did, she was giving me the same look that Nala gave Simba in *The Lion King* when he finally pinned her down.

In that moment, I wanted her bad as fuck!

We were supposed to be taking our time, though, and I didn't want to mess up by rushing it. *This taking it slow shit is hard!* I tried to mentally shake it off.

"You wanna go grab something to eat?"

"I'd like that," Melody replied, entwining her fingers with mine.

We walked hand in hand, making more comfortable conversation as we made our way back to my car. It felt good. She felt good.

We decided on Waffle House, opting to have breakfast for dinner. She promised to make me an omelet in the near future that would make me swoon.

"You'll never want Waffle House again," she stated confidently.

"I can't wait," I told her before taking a bite of my ham and cheese omelet.

The evening progressed, and she shared tales of her youth. I even threw in a tale or two about my wild adolescent years. I was a little apprehensive about telling her the bits and pieces of my troubled childhood, but she looked at me with an expression of wonder on her face.

"What?" I wanted to know after she stared at me for a moment.

"You impress me," Melody simply replied.

"Me?" I said with a laugh. "I haven't done anything special."

"You are special," she offered. "You've been through a

lot. I can tell. But, here you are, a successful barber, a mom, and making things happen for yourself. You're more than just a survivor of your circumstance. You prevail and excel, and I think that's nothing short of amazing."

I felt my face grow warm at her compliment.

"Thank you," I told her quietly, humbled.

"Thank you for sharing with me," she said, smiling at me. "It's getting easier, isn't it?"

I smiled back at her before returning my attention to my food.

Yeah, it's getting easier.

The ride home was a relaxed one. We rode with the windows down and the music turned up as the sun started to set. Every now and then, she would sing along with whatever song was playing. I felt like I could listen to her sing for the rest of my life.

After pulling into my driveway, I escorted her to her front door. Still determined to take things slow, I leaned forward and kissed her on the lips.

"I'm trying to end this date the right way," I told her. "So, this is the part where I tell you goodnight."

"No," she said, shaking her head. "If you really want to end this date right, this is the part where you come inside with me."

FINALLY

My heart was beating a tattoo into my chest as Melody took my hand and led me into her house. My nerves were on edge. I couldn't remember the last time I had been nervous about being with a woman, but my stomach was damn near churning. I wasn't prepared. My bag of goodies was at my house, and it didn't look like she was going to give me the chance to go and get it.

As I followed her into the living room, I watched as she let go of my hand and went to slide the coffee table away from her sofa. She motioned for me to sit on the floor in front of her loveseat.

"Get comfortable," Melody said with a sensual smile. "I'm about to slip into something a little more comfortable. Then, I will be back."

I watched her strut away, and it took everything in my power not to follow her into her bedroom. But, I was determined to do this the right way, or at least as close to the right way as possible. I stepped out of my shoes and placed them on the side of the loveseat before making myself comfortable on the plush carpet as requested.

Though it had only been a couple minutes, it felt like hours had gone by while I waited for Melody to return. When she did, she caught me completely off guard.

Dressed in an oversized t-shirt and a pair of fuzzy house shoes, she walked over to where I sat and took a seat on the floor a couple of feet opposite of me. After positioning herself to sit Indian style, she held up her hand.

I couldn't stop the laugh that escaped from my throat as I laid eyes on a fresh deck of Uno cards.

"You play too damn much," I chuckled.

"Are you ready for this ass whoopin' or what?" she asked with mock impatience.

"Do you mean the one I'm about to put on you?" I shot back.

"Come get some," she challenged as she opened the deck.

I had been wrapped up in my nerves, and she came in and put me at complete ease just by being her silly self. Maybe she had been nervous, too, and figure it would be better to diffuse the tension that had become thick as molasses between us from the moment we kissed in the garden.

As we played, I couldn't stop looking at her. I could tell by the look in her eyes that she wanted me as much as I wanted her. I could taste the desire on her lips. But, we were determined to take our time with this.

However, my patience was already wearing thin. I longed to touch her.

"What?" she asked, flashing a shy smile.

"You're beautiful."

I saw her cheeks deepen. I loved that shit.

"Thank you," she said quietly.

"Come here."

I don't think she knew how sexy she looked crawling over to me. I could barely keep my composure as she came closer. She paused in front of me for a second before settling herself in a position so that she was facing me with her legs on either side of me. It would have been so easy to touch her, but I refrained.

She looked at me, her face full of curiosity and something else. Maybe it was expectation.

I touched her face. "Baby, you're making this so hard for me," I confessed. "I'm really trying to do this the right way."

"And what's the right way?" she whispered before biting her bottom lip, which turned me on even more.

I chuckled, but my laugh was mirthless.

"I don't know," I answered with a shrug. "I just want this shit to be right."

"I do, too," she said quietly. "So what do we do now?"

"I'm going to kiss you," I answered. "Then, I'm going to go home and take a cold shower."

She was quiet for a moment, but what she said while linking her arms at the back of my neck changed everything.

"I don't want you to go."

"Then I'll stay."

The fragment of resolve I had left was completely lost as I pulled her closer to me. Our lips joined as if we'd both been starving for each other.

I can't speak for her, but I think I *was* starving. And, damn, her mouth was delectable. I wanted to taste the rest of her.

She let out a soft moan when my lips traveled to her neck. Her hands gripped my shoulders as my hands went for the hem of her shirt. I grabbed handfuls of the cotton material and worked it towards her waist. She assisted by raising her ass off the floor so I could pull the shirt from beneath her. The groan that escaped my throat was a blend of agony and delight.

She wore no panties underneath.

"Really, baby?" I croaked into her neck.

"I wanted to be prepared just in case," she cooed with a pleased chuckle.

She gasped when I released the material of the shirt and filled my hands with the flesh of her ass instead.

"You're so fuckin' soft," I uttered in amazement.

I let my hands roam from her ass to the smooth skin of her back, only to find she wasn't wearing a bra either.

"What the fuck are you trying to do to me, lady?" I demanded, unable to keep my hands off her.

"Well, I wanted the set to match," she joked, giggling as I nibbled on the delicate skin below her ear.

This shit was killing me.

I reached for the hem of her shirt again, pulling it over her head this time.

For a moment, I could only look at her. Her cocoa-hued skin was flawless and made me wonder how it was possible for skin to be so beautiful. I took in every inch of flesh my eyes could allow. When my gaze reached her face, she looked away from me.

"What's wrong?" I wanted to know.

"I don't look anything like your ex," she began. "She's all pretty and slim, and I'm a size sixteen-"

"First of all," I interrupted her, turning her face so she could look at me and see I wasn't bullshitting with her, "this is our space, our time. I didn't invite my ex into your house, and you don't do it, either. There's no room in here for her. Second, I don't give a fuck what size you wear. You're fuckin' beautiful, and I'm crazy as hell about you. So, quit trippin' over nonsense and bring those lips to me."

A smile crept across her lips before she did as I instructed.

It had only been moments since we'd kissed, but our tongues danced as if it had been forever. I knew right then that I could kiss her for forever and never get tired of it.

Still holding on to her, I rose from where I sat and gently laid her back onto the carpet.

She looked at me through lowered eyelids. "Touch me, Jazz," she invited.

"Don't worry, love," I told her. "I will."

Though the idea of not rushing into this part of this new relationship had been blown to hell, I still wanted to take my time with loving her. I wanted to make every touch worth remembering, every kiss worthy of daydreaming about, and every taste permanently burned into our brains.

I kissed her slowly and deeply while positioning my clothed body over her naked one. I felt her wrap one leg around my waist as she held on to me. Unable to resist, I began to roll my hips, slowly grinding against her exposed flesh. When she whimpered into my mouth, I felt my restraint being chipped away.

I pulled my lips away from hers and traveled to the side of her neck. I teased her skin with the tip of my tongue before kissing and gently sucking on the delicate skin just below her ear. I slowly worked my way downward, leaving a trail of kisses from her neck to her collarbone to her breasts, taking my time to enjoy each Hershey Kiss-colored nipple as she squirmed beneath me.

As I sampled her left breast, I allowed my hand to travel down to the cavern nestled between her thighs. I slid my fingers between the folds that hid the jewel I'd only fantasized about before. She was slick, warm, and ready for me to touch her. She moaned and arched her back as I began to leisurely massage her clitoris.

"Finally," she wailed in delight as she rotated her hips in accord with my fingers.

She moaned again as I slid my fingers inside of her. "Ooh," she cooed, her pleasure evident.

But, I was just getting started.

I continued kissing my way down her body. I tried to touch every bit of her skin with my lips before going down to her thighs. She was ready for me and I knew it, but I wasn't going to give it to her so easily. I kissed her inner thighs, taking my time to go old school and leave a mark on her right thigh that only she and I could see. I continued my path until I'd kissed every visible part of her from her neck to her toes. She laughed hard when I softly bit her big toe.

Pleased that I had found one of her sensitive spots, I stored that information in the back of my mind for future use before deliberately traveling back up to the center of her body. Unhurriedly, I ran the tip of my tongue up and down the slit that concealed the clit awaiting the same treatment.

She groaned. The sound was a blend of pleasure and agony. I felt her hands on my head. Her fingers flexed against my short hair as if she were fighting the urge to pull me into her. I finally obliged her, taking my fingers and spreading her lips apart to let my tongue slide inside.

I think we both fucking moaned at the initial contact, her from pleasure and I from hunger.

I'd be lying if I said I didn't have experience putting my mouth on one of the most sensitive parts of the female anatomy. I'd even like to think if ranked, I would be at the expert or master level. I've dove in and damn near consumed souls, but never had I been consumed.

Until now.

It felt like waves of warm water flowed over my entire body. I wondered what the hell "they" had put in the water she drank. Had her body been purified in the Fountain of

Youth? I didn't know what it was, but I was in heaven.

I let the taste of her wash over me again and again. Hearing her moan over and over again only intensified my appetite and thirst for her. I was enchanted by the experience.

And I had formed an instant bond with her clit. I wrote the ABC's in cursive with my tongue. I dotted my "I's" and "J's" and crossed my "T's" I signed my name all over it.

"Jazz!" she called out, gripping the back of my head.

Knowing she was about to come, my manipulations became more intense.

"Oh… My… God."

She forced the words out of her mouth as I continued to lap and lash at her wetness, taking in every bit I could. I could've died in that moment and been completely content with it.

She cried out again as another wave flowed over her. She writhed uncontrollably, her hips rising to meet my mouth. She offered me every ounce of her, and I drank from her well greedily. I licked, sampled, and devoured her until she couldn't take it anymore, and even then, I worked until I got one more orgasm out of her.

Afterwards, she curled into the fetal position and trembled.

I lay down on the floor behind her and spooned her. I wrapped my arm around her and kissed the back of her neck. She held my arm in place for a minute.

"Are you good?" I whispered to her while smiling to myself, feeling a little cocky.

Her reply killed that.

"No," she whispered back, then released my hand and turned her head slightly to make sure I could hear her. "I need for you to go home."

"Home?" I asked, surprised. "But I thought-"

She held up a finger and hushed me. "I need for you to go home. Now. Please."

Well. This shit was completely unexpected.

I was completely thrown off. I had just made her come several times over, brought tears to her eyes, and made her ass curl up in a fucking fetal position. Now she was sending me home?

I was in shock. I didn't know what to say. I was at a total loss.

Before I said or did something I would regret, I got up from the floor, put on my shoes, and walked out of her house to go to my own.

Confused, I stopped halfway between our homes and almost turned around to ask her what the fuck was wrong with her and what did I do wrong, but I caught myself. What I wasn't going to do was go back to look like a damn fool.

There I was earlier that damn day, admitting to myself that I was in love with her. Now I was walking home after she sent me away.

I unlocked my door and went inside. I removed my shoes at the door and left them right there. Then, I went into my kitchen to grab a beer. I could still taste her on my tongue, and I hoped the drink would wash her essence away.

It didn't work. After taking two long gulps, I gave up.

My doorbell rang as I walked out of the kitchen. Not even looking through the peephole first, I opened the door.

There she stood in a robe with no shoes on.

"Did I forget something?" I asked with a raised eyebrow.

"Yes," she answered, untying the robe right there on my porch. "Me."

OFFICIAL

The smell of eggs, ham, and a variety of vegetables being sautéed filled the air. I leaned against the counter, watching her work.

She was dressed in one of my t-shirts, and I couldn't help but admire how those pretty cheeks peeked from just below the hem, teasing me. It had only been a couple of hours since my hands had been filled with them.

Remembering how soft she felt revived my desire for her. As I watched her, I wanted her even more than I had when she stepped into my home and kissed me.

Melody was throwing my life off balance. Or maybe she was just restructuring it.

In one night, she'd sent me through a myriad of emotions. Love, lust, disbelief, maybe even a dash of sadness and anger. Then, she gave me love again blended with passion.

I was beside myself when she'd sent me home. I dare to even say I was more than a little hurt and confused by it. But, then, she was at my front door.

She had come to me.

"Did you think we were done?" she teased me.

For a moment, I couldn't form a thought. I could only stare at her as the light from my front porch highlighted the beautiful brown flesh that was exposed through her open robe.

My God! She was sexy as fuck in that moment.

She stepped inside, not waiting for an invitation, and wrapped her arms around my neck. She pulled me to her so she could combine her lips with mine.

I welcomed her tongue's invasion into my mouth. Then, I met her the rest of the way, wrapping my arms around her waist and pulling her even closer to me. Not even air could get between us.

I was greedy as I drank from her mouth. Our tongues mated, dancing sensually against each other in a rhythm only our souls could create. I looked at her after relinquishing her lips.

"You play too fuckin' much," I told her.

She chuckled. "Were you worried or something?" she asked, trying to look innocent.

"I think you already know the answer to that," I replied as my hands dove inside of her robe.

I grabbed handfuls of her ass, loving how it was firm yet soft.

"Gotdamn, you feel so fuckin' good. Don't scare me like that again."

She chuckled again. "I just needed a moment to recuperate," she confessed. "I mean, you did have me curled up on the floor like a baby."

"You didn't have to send me home, though. Shit!"

"Oh, we needed to come here anyway," she said, purring as she nuzzled up to me. "I told you we aren't done."

Then, she took me by the hand and led me to my own damn bedroom.

As I thought about the way Melody moaned when I feasted on her only hours before, I found myself walking over to hold her from behind. I kissed her on the neck as she stirred the mixed veggies in a skillet. She giggled; the sound was music to my ears.

My hand journeyed downward, and my fingers slid between her pussy lips. She moaned lightly as I massaged her gently.

"You're gonna make me burn the food," she fussed weakly. Even as she spoke, she leaned back against me.

"Then I could just have you for breakfast," I said against her neck.

My fingers became more persistent and she dropped the spatula, forgetting about the food for a moment. It went ignored as it hit the floor. I felt her hand rest on top of mine before she began to gently coerce my fingers deeper inside.

I was ready to say fuck the food, but it was my cellphone that made us pause.

It rang out Lyric's ringtone. I had to answer it.

"That's Lyric," I explained with a sigh.

She smiled her understanding. "Well, get it, love."

As I walked away, throwing a tiny tantrum, she laughed and bent down to pick up the utensil.

"She just saved our breakfast anyway," Melody said. "Tell her I said good morning."

I answered my phone. "Good morning, kid," I greeted.

"Good morning!" she said cheerfully. "Did you and Mel have a good time yesterday?"

If only you knew.

"Yes, we did," I replied. "How's it going for you with JB, Nelle, and Kayla?"

"I'm having fun," she answered. "Kay-Kay is so cute, and she follows me everywhere. She keeps trying to play on my phone, though."

As I listened to my daughter give the details of her first sleepover, I watched Melody step out of the kitchen with a platter of food in one hand and a bowl of fruit in the other. As good as the food smelled, the only thing I wanted to put my mouth on was the woman who had cooked it.

"Auntie Nelle told me to ask you if you wanted them to bring me home or if you wanted to pick me up later."

I returned my attention to my daughter. "Tell her either way is fine with me."

I heard Lyric yell my response to Shanelle.

"Tell her that we'll be there in about an hour!" I heard Shanelle yell back.

"She said-"

"I heard her," I interrupted with a chuckle. "I'm glad you're having a good time. See you in a little bit, shorty."

"Okay," she said. "See you later!"

"Later, boo," I told her before ending the call.

I joined Melody at the table she set for us. I looked down at the breakfast that she had prepared for me, which included a huge omelet filled with ham, several cheeses, and a ton of vegetables. Then, I looked over at the bowl of fresh strawberries, pineapple chucks, and cantaloupe that she picked from.

"That's all you're eating?" I asked, while reaching for my fork.

"This is all I want," she replied. "Foodwise, I mean."

I looked at her; she was giving me that look again.

"You're gonna have to stop looking at me like that," I warned her. "Fuck around and this food will be left on this damn table."

She laughed and picked up a pineapple chunk. "My bad."

"Uh huh," I said, then took my first bite of the omelet.

It was sin on a fork.

"Jesus, girl," I began, savoring the food as it virtually melted in my mouth. "Who taught you how to cook? Why aren't you at somebody's restaurant as head chef?"

"I'm glad you like it," she said with a pleased grin.

"I love it," I told her. "This is so good. You have many gifts."

She blushed and I had to catch my breath. Beautiful voice, great cook, wonderful lover, and she adored my daughter. She was wifey material.

My stomach flipped at the thought.

Get it together, Jazz. Just because you had phenomenal sex doesn't mean it's time to let your imagination run away with you. It's way too soon for these kinds of thoughts.

I tried to shake it off, but the feeling kept coming back.

I returned my attention to my plate and savored the breakfast she'd taken the time to whip up for me. I looked up at her just in time to see her lick the juice from a strawberry from her bottom lip. I was hit with a ton of memories from the night before.

The taste of her…

The surprise I felt when she confessed she wanted to do the same for me…

The bigger surprise for me when she turned out to be good as fuck at it…

Flipping her over and making her cry out when I licked her from behind before sliding inside of her…

Gripping her waist as I stroked her from behind…

The pleasure I felt as she threw it back on me...

She was soft, giving, and confident in the bed. She knew when to be submissive and when to take control. I damn near bit my tongue as I remembered how she mounted up and rode the fuck out of the dick.

She was fucking perfect. I'd met my match.

She looked at me and blushed. I knew I was staring, but damn. In that moment, it hit me again that I was in love with her.

"Share," she requested.

I wasn't ready to hit her with that truth. So, instead, I replied, "I think you're amazing."

I didn't think it was possible, but her blush deepened.

"So are you," she replied bashfully.

I smiled at her and she smiled back.

This was some real Kodak or Hallmark type shit, but with the bonus of some good-ass sex mixed in. I wanted her again but had to remind myself that Lyric would be home soon.

As if reading my mind, she spoke.

"What are we going to tell Lyric about us?"

"I'm not sure yet," I answered. "It's not like she's not used to seeing us together already."

"True," she replied. "But what if I want to kiss you? How do you think she'll react?"

I thought about it for a moment. "I have no idea. I've never been in this type of situation before."

"Situation?" Melody asked with a raised eyebrow. "What kind of situation are you in, pray tell?"

"Being with someone and having my daughter," I answered. "This will be my first relationship with someone while my daughter is living with me. Hell, this will be my first relationship in a long time, period."

She took a bite out of a strawberry, then stood up. For a second, she just stared at me. Then, a slow smile spread across her face as she walked over to me.

She bent down and kissed me on my lips before asking, "So are we in a relationship? Is this thing between us official?"

I thought about her question for a moment. Once upon a time, a question like that would have been an automatic termination of communication between me and a woman. I had deemed myself allergic to that kind of shit. However, as I looked up at Melody standing in front of me and wearing my shirt as if she did it every day, I wanted to be cured of my allergy.

"Yeah," I finally answered. "Yeah, I think it is."

Her smile was brighter than the sun as she came closer to kiss me again. This time, I adjusted myself in my chair and pulled her into my lap.

I savored the taste of the strawberry on her tongue as she wrapped her arms around me and held me tighter. I looked forward to more mornings like this. My hands crept beneath the t-shirt so I could caress the skin of her back. She moaned softly as I gently ran my nails down her spine. She giggled a little as she arched her back in response.

Yes, I'm going to enjoy having this in my life.

When she pulled away from me, her voice was sultry as hell when she spoke. "How long do we have before Lyric comes home?"

"Long enough," I answered as we both stood to our feet to head to the bedroom.

The rest of breakfast went forgotten as my girlfriend and I finished our morning off feasting on each other and consummating our relationship.

After years of running from relationships, I, Jazz "The Playboi" Richardson, had a real-deal girlfriend.

And I already loved her.

A FAMILY THING

"You can tell me I'm right now."

"I don't know what you're talking about."

"Shit, bruh. You're glowing and shit. I ain't *ever* seen you glow."

I laughed at my best friend as we sat at a table in the mall drinking a couple of fountain drinks. The ladies were off getting manicures and pedicures.

It had only been two weeks since Melody and I made our relationship official, but it felt like we'd been together longer. Though we still hadn't said anything to Lyric about it, I think she picked up on it. To anyone on the outside looking in, we looked like we'd been a family for years.

"I don't know what you're talking about, homie," I said to my friend, although I couldn't help but laugh.

"You know," JB began, "it's absolutely okay to admit I was right about this. Come on… admit it."

After a moment, I replied, "Okay, you *might've* been on to something. But, that's all you're getting from me!"

She laughed victoriously. "I'll take that! I know that was hard for you, but I'm still gonna gloat about it. I knew it was destiny just from you guys' names."

"Destiny?" I chuckled. "That may be stretching it a bit."

"No!" she argued. "Peep this. Jazz, Melody, and Lyric. It's

a trifecta! I can already see a family holiday card with y'all picture, Christmas tree, and musical notes and shit!"

We both laughed.

"You are mentally challenged, bitch," I told her, but I did smile at the imagery.

"See," she said. "There's that glow again. My best friend is in love!"

"Stop that shit," I demanded firmly, but I was losing the battle with the smile that was trying to take over my face.

"You know you still owe me though," she then said. Her face went somber as she made the statement.

"What do you mean?" I asked, confused for a moment.

"Lyric," she replied. "you never told me what the deal was. I mean, we're supposed to be best friends. How did I not know that you had a whole kid? I can't even say that it doesn't fuck with me a little bit. After watching me go through everything I went through when I found out about Nelle being pregnant. You probably could've given me some insight and help me through it, but you didn't say a thing."

I thought hard before I answered.

"There really want much for me to say, to be honest," I told her. I tried to be careful with my words as I continued. "Hell, I was trying to fight being triggered by it myself. I remember seeing Shanelle while she was pregnant. She was beautiful and happy, and she had that pregnancy glow that you always hear about. She looked like the model for the perfect fucking pregnancy. My shit went nothing like that."

My friend listened intently as I spoke. While being this open made me uncomfortable, I knew my friend deserved to know. I pushed on. "I was a kid, virtually homeless, and didn't have anybody to go to. I was self-medicating and the biggest fucking weed head I knew and there I was knocked up and scared as hell. I'd thought about having an abortion and even went to the clinic but I couldn't go through with it. But I knew I couldn't take care of a baby. All I knew was babies needed to be loved and I didn't have the capacity for it. I ain't know shit about love and I wasn't going to put a baby through what I had been through. I would rather have died than do that anyone." I took a breath and continued. "I found my old case worker, hoping that she could help me. She went above and beyond, letting me stay with her and her husband. I figured she'd probably help me with putting the baby up for adoption, but she surprised me."

"How so?" J.B. wanted to know.

"She offered to take care of her until I was ready for her," I answered. "She told me she had faith in me and she would take care of my daughter until I was in the position to take care of her. We'd kept in contact over the years, but she wanted me to focus on really getting myself together, so I did. She called me a couple of months ago, and here we are now. I'm a full-time mama."

"I wouldn't have ever imagined this shit," J.B. confessed, shaking her head.

"Hell, me either!" I replied with a chuckle. "I didn't think I'd ever be ready. But I'm learning bit by bit and I wouldn't trade her for anything. I'm still figuring stuff out and sometimes it seems like she closer to Melody-"

"Yeah," J.B. interrupted. "Then there's her. She's a whole other subject."

"Right," I agreed, shaking my head in awe. "She something else."

"It's okay to be happy, Jazz," she said. "I mean that real-deal shit. Enjoy it."

"I can't even lie," I confessed. "She keeps a smile on my

face."

"I can see that," JB said, nodding in approval. "I knew you had a thing for her the first time I met her. I'm glad I was right. You two are a good look. It was overdue for you."

"Maybe," I conceded.

"So," JB began, clearing her throat as if she was about to touch on a serious topic.

I waited.

"Y'all fuck yet?"

I laughed. Hard.

"I wouldn't call it that," I answered slowly, thinking.

"So what would you call it?" my friend asked, intrigued.

"I dunno," I returned. "I don't know what to call it, but it was more than fuckin'."

I sat back for a minute, instantly reliving the kisses, the touches, her taste, her damn mouth work, and how she put it on me.

"Hey, hey, hey," JB said, snapping her fingers. "Come back to earth."

I refocused on my friend and we both laughed again.

"Yeah, she's got you all fucked up."

As JB called me out, I looked up and smiled. It looked like she was moving in slow motion. Her face, her smile, her curves, her thickness… All of that was mine.

"Yeah," I told my friend. "That's my baby."

We greeted our women and daughters as they approached the table. I smiled at Lyric as she showed me her freshly polished nails and toes. I looked at JB and saw the joy on her face as her youngster showed off her pink nails.

I finally understood how she felt. And I liked it.

I looked up at Melody, and she smiled back at me.

I had a feeling this beautiful woman was going to change

my life in a big way.

* * * *
*

"Are you nervous?"

"A little bit, but I'll be okay."

I looked at Lyric as she fidgeted with her little purse. I then looked over at Melody who was watching her, also. She looked up at me and mouthed, *She's nervous.* I nodded in agreement.

We sat quietly and waited for the principal of the school to begin her greeting for Lyric's new school's orientation.

"Good evening, parents and students. I'm Mrs. Evans, and I am the school principal. We are so glad to have you all here this evening…"

I watched my daughter look intently at the principal, taking in every word that the woman shared. I marveled at her intellect and her eagerness to prove she was a big girl who was not afraid of yet another change in her life.

After the welcome from the principal, we were able to tour the school and meet her teacher.

"Good evening," she greeted, shaking my hand first and then Melody's. "I'm Mrs. Davis. I'm one of the fifth grade teachers here. Are you her parents?"

I looked at Melody, who smiled and gave me a discreet nod. I couldn't help but to smile back.

"Yes, ma'am," I then replied proudly to the teacher. "I'm Jasmine Richardson, and this is Melody."

"It's a pleasure to meet you," she said before turning her attention to Lyric. She looked at her and smiled before speaking. "I haven't seen you around here before, so I'm guessing you're new. What's your name, young lady?"

"Lyric Richardson," my daughter replied solemnly. "And yes, ma'am, I'm new."

"Well, Miss Richardson, we're going to have a great year!"

Mrs. Davis talked to Lyric for a few minutes before telling us that she looked forward to spending the next nine months with her. She then excused herself to meet another family.

I could tell she put my daughter at ease.

"So what do you think?" I asked her.

"I think I'm going to like Mrs. Davis."

"I'm glad to hear that!" I told her.

"Do you think you're going be alright?" Melody asked.

"I think so," Lyric answered. "I'm kinda excited now."

As we walked to the parking lot, Lyric asked a question that shocked both of us.

"Are you both my parents now?"

Melody and I stopped in our tracks and looked at my daughter.

"When Mrs. Davis asked if you were my parents, you said yes."

Unbothered, she continued towards the car. Before getting in, she turned around, looked at Melody, and said, "If you want to be one of my parents, I'm okay with it. I think it would be cool to have two moms."

She then climbed into the car and waited for us to do the same.

We looked at each other, both surprised and amused that Lyric had so easily voiced her opinion.

I wasn't sure if she understood the dynamics of my relationship with Melody just yet. We still hadn't told her that we had officially become an item. However, that didn't seem to matter. Lyric already knew what she wanted, and she had no problem saying it.

As we got in the car, I had to admit to myself that I really did like the sound of it.

*   *   *   *
*

The beep from the microwave signaled that the first bag of popcorn was ready.

"I'll get it!" Lyric yelled as she jumped up from where she sat on the floor. She ran into Melody's kitchen to remove one bag of Redenbacher's best pour-over popcorn from the microwave and replace it with another.

"Be careful," Melody called out to her.

She had promised Lyric an all-night movie night before she started school, and it was time to pay up.

"You're gonna be tired tomorrow," I told Melody as we watched Lyric run off. "Aren't you going to church in the morning?"

We were on the sofa. I was sitting, and she was laid out with her head resting on a throw pillow in my lap.

"I'll be fine," she replied. "I promised her this, and I'm gonna see it through." She was quiet for a minute before speaking again. "You guys wanna come with me tomorrow?"

"Come where?" Lyric yelled from the kitchen.

"Church," Melody answered back.

"Ooh!" my daughter said in excitement. "I wanna go! I went every Sunday with Nana and Pop. I even got to sing in the youth choir!"

"I didn't know that," I said as she came back into the living room. "You can sing, too?"

"Maybe not as good as Mel," she replied, "but they let me

lead two songs at church."

Her chest puffed up with pride. I still had so much to learn about my daughter.

"Are you going to sing, Mel?" she asked. I could hear the hope in her voice.

"I might," Melody answered, basking in the child's admiration.

"Can we go?" my daughter pleaded with me. "Pleeeeease!"

I hadn't been to a church service since my grandmother passed away. Now, I believe in a higher power, and I even kept the bible my grandmother gave me that I occasionally read scriptures from. But, that was about as far as I went with religion. I never felt comfortable with the idea of going to church. I had come across quite a few not-so-Christlike Christians in my lifetime, and it deterred me from wanting to enter that holy building.

However, as I looked at my daughter who was almost bouncing with anticipation, and I saw the glimmer of hope in Melody's eyes, I gave in.

"Sure. We can go."

"Yay!"

I couldn't help but smile a little at their combined joy. It made me feel good to know they at least wanted me there.

"So are you gonna wear a dress?" my daughter asked, catching me completely off guard.

"A dress?" I repeated, dumbfounded as hell. "I don't think so."

"Have you ever worn a dress?" she then asked, taking a seat on the recliner and looking at me in fascination.

"A long time ago when I was younger than you," I answered with a chuckle.

"Have you ever worn makeup before?" she questioned.

"Nope," I replied. "Never."

Melody sat up and looked at me. "Never?"

"Nope," I replied, shaking my head.

"I bet you'd look real pretty," Lyric said.

I could see the wheels spinning in her head. When I looked over at Melody, I could tell from her expression that her train was on the same track as my daughter's.

"Oh, no!" I said, jumping up. "Don't even think about it!"

They both jumped up with me.

"Awww, come on!"

"It'll be fun!"

"Fun for who?" I argued back.

"Please, Ma!" Lyric begged.

"Y'all are not about to put that goo on my face!"

About thirty minutes later, I was sitting in the dining room waiting for Melody to pass me a mirror. I felt nervous as I looked at my girlfriend and daughter's faces. Their smiles were way too big for my comfort. I prayed they didn't have me looking like a damn clown.

They had discussed what colors to use, what kind of blush, whether or not to contour -whatever the hell that was, and whether to go with a matte lipstick or a gloss. My anxiety grew a little as Lyric giggled with glee as they worked. My anxiety grew a lot when Melody disappeared and came back with the finishing touch…a damn wig.

"Y'all are just eatin' this shit up, huh?" I asked, trying not to be a party pooper since my ladies seemed to be having so much fun.

"Yes!" Melody answered with a pleased laugh as she situated the synthetic hair on my scalp. "We might not ever get this chance again!"

"Oh, I can just about guarantee that shit," I told them.

They just laughed and continued on as if I hadn't spoken. I rolled my eyes as she primped and played with the hair to get it just how she wanted it. Then to add insult to injury, she finished the look off by pulling one side of the hair back and pinning it with a rhinestone hair clip.

They both stepped back and looked at me as if they had magically transformed me. Melody smiled and shook her head in disbelief while Lyric bounced up and down, barely able to contain herself.

"Oh my God," Melody said, still looking at me in awe. It almost made me uncomfortable. "You are so pretty!"

Lyric bobbed her head enthusiastically in agreement.

"Well, can I see now?" I wanted to see what the fuss was all about.

Melody disappeared again and came back with the mirror.

After taking the mirror from her, I took a deep breath and held it up to inspect their work.

"Oh, shit!"

I wasn't pretty. I was fine as hell! I didn't even recognize myself. I mean, I saw me, but I couldn't see me. I was completely surprised.

I can't even front. My girls had done a great job, and I let them know as much.

"So, okay, okay. I'm cute as hell."

They laughed.

As I looked at myself again in the mirror, I saw the flash of light and immediately looked up. Lyric looked like she got caught with her hand in the cookie jar.

"Really?" I said incredulously.

"You just look so pretty," she told me. "And you already said this wouldn't happen again. So, I wanted at least one picture to remember this."

She was so matter-of-fact about it that it tugged at my heartstrings.

"Come here," I told her. When she came to me, I took her phone out of her hand, pulled her close to my side, and held the phone up. "Selfie?"

She hugged me, and it warmed my entire soul. She leaned in and smiled. I smiled with her and took the picture. She looked at it and nodded her approval. She then showed it to Melody.

"Send me a copy," Melody said with a chuckle.

"This better not end up on the internet," I warned them. I then looked at Melody and asked, "Can I get a towel to wash my face now?"

As Melody walked away, I looked at my daughter and found her staring at me.

"What?"

"You just look so different," she answered.

I sat there for a moment before asking, "Is this how you would rather see me every day?"

I held my breath while waiting for her response.

"No, ma'am," she answered. "It would be too weird. This was fun, but I like you the way you are."

Her simple statement nearly overwhelmed me. *I love this little girl.*

"Thank you."

By the time we were in the middle of the second movie, Lyric had fallen asleep on the floor. Melody rose from the sofa and got her up before escorting her to the guest bedroom. She then came back to the sofa and reached her hand out to me. I took it and followed her to her bedroom.

We made love, struggling to keep quiet so we didn't wake Lyric. Later, we laid in the bed cuddled up, almost out of there. I pulled her closer to me. She entwined her fingers with mine and surprised me by kissing my hand.

"Thank you for tonight," she whispered to me sleepily. "It was fun."

"My pleasure, baby girl," I replied before diving into the waters headfirst. "I love you, Mel."

It wasn't necessarily an overture or some grand proclamation or anything, but I wanted her to know. I didn't want to keep holding it in.

"I love you, too, Jazz," she replied softly. I could hear the smile in her voice. "Now go to sleep. We have church in a couple of hours."

And that was that.

It had been so simple.

And it felt so damn good.

I fell asleep, sure that I could take on anything in the world as long as I had her by my side.

With her and my daughter in my life, I felt something I don't recall ever feeling.

Like I had a family all my own.

GUESS WHO'S COMING TO DINNER

I don't think there had been a time in my life when everything felt perfect. I'm not going to pretend that my life hadn't gotten better by leaps and bounds over the past years, but it never felt like this. I had never been this happy before.

Business was booming, and me and my co-workers were finally looking into a building of our own. I had a smart, beautiful, funny daughter who had blossomed and was opening up to me more with each passing day. I had a beautiful woman who loved me as much as I loved her. Hell, I was even in good with her folks and went to church with them all on occasion. Lyric went every Sunday. The Kings welcomed her as if Melody had given birth to her herself.

I had absolutely no complaints. Everything was perfect.

"Lyric, are you almost ready?" I yelled out, while looking at my reflection in the mirror.

"I'm ready," she answered, walking into my bedroom.

She looked cute in her Thanksgiving outfit and freshly done braids.

"You look pretty," I told her.

She smiled, always loving getting compliments. "So do you," she replied back.

"Thank you," I told her before grabbing my keys from my dresser. "Let's go then."

The drive to the Kings' house was lively. Lyric kept the conversation going talking about things happening at her school and her new friend Anjella.

We pulled up to the Kings' house and found several cars, including Melody's, parked in the front of the large abode. After parking on the street, we made our way up the driveway to the front door and rang the bell. Melody's mother answered the door.

"Hey, my babies," she greeted, giving me and Lyric kisses on our cheeks. "Y'all come on in. Everything is almost ready. We're just waiting on my brother to get here."

She inched us further into the living room where several relatives were sitting. A few guys were watching a football game, including Melody's father who smiled and waved at us.

"Hey, girls," he said jovially. "Come on in and make yourselves at home!"

"Everybody," Mrs. King called out to the visitors, "this is Jazz and Little Miss Lyric. They belong to Melody. Jazz and Lyric, this is the family!"

Warmed by the introduction, I said hello to the group.

"Lyric, a couple of the kids are in the backyard if you want to go outside," Mrs. King suggested, then turned to me. "Mel is in the kitchen if you're looking for her."

"Thank you," I told her with a grin before following her into the kitchen where I found Melody pulling sweet Hawaiian rolls out of the oven.

"Hey!" she said with a huge smile.

She set the rolls on the countertop, then walked over and gave me a hug as if she didn't just see me the day before.

"Hey, baby," I whispered in her ear.

"Hey, Mel!" Lyric chimed in, waving as she made her way to the kitchen door to go outside.

"Hey, boo," Melody answered before turning back to me to give me a quick peck on my lips.

"Behave," I scolded her, but I was grinning from ear to ear. "Your mama and aunties are right there."

"Oh, they know what the deal is," she retorted, sashaying back to the counter to transfer the rolls from the pan to a container so they could be put on the table that they had set up buffet-style.

"Do you need help with anything?" I offered, following her to the table.

"No," she replied. "We got this."

She fixed me a drink, and I was formally introduced to some of the family members.

"Arnez is running a little behind, but he's on the way," Mrs. King announced to the family. "Somebody go and tell the kids to wash their hands. We're gonna go ahead and get started with dinner."

She didn't have to say it twice. Everyone rose to their feet to get ready for Thanksgiving dinner. After Mr. King prayed over the food, the kids were fed first to get them out of the way. Then, wives started making plates for their husbands.

I smiled when Melody got in line to make my plate. She really didn't have to, but I appreciated the gesture. It spoke volumes. As I watched her, I fiddled with the velvet box in my pocket. It had only been a few months, but I felt in my heart that she was *the one*. Tonight, I wanted to let her know in front of her entire family.

"What?" she whispered with a smile while we ate.

I didn't realize I had been staring at her until she spoke.

"You are so beautiful."

She blushed and looked at me through lowered eyelids. "Thank you," she said shyly.

It tickled me that I could still get that reaction out of her.

"I love you," I told her then.

"I love you, too," she said, looking me in my eyes.

I could hardly wait for the surprise I had in store for her.

"What are you two lovebirds talking about over there?" her mother asked with a knowing smile.

Before either of us could say anything, her expression changed to one of delight.

"Arnez!"

She jumped up from where she sat and ran towards the entryway of the dining room. We watched as she jumped into the arms of the man who stood there. Murmurs of happiness and boisterous salutations filled the air as the family bid their greetings to the newest arrival.

"That's Uncle Arnie," Melody informed me before standing up to run over to give her uncle a hug.

Everyone seemed thrilled to see him, and I was looking forward to meeting him…

Until I saw his face.

It felt like my heart stopped beating. Then, it went into overdrive.

It was a face I could never erase, no matter how hard I tried.

Time had been good to him. He almost looked the same, just way cleaner. Gone were the flashy clothes and big jewelry. They had been replaced by a nice looking off-the-rack suit. The smile was the same, and he flashed it at his family with ease, his joy at seeing them apparent.

When his eyes fell on me, I saw a flicker in them. It was like a question was momentarily written in them. *Do I know you?*

I looked away, temporarily forgetting how to breathe.

Inhale, Jazz. Exhale, Jazz. Repeat…

I looked up again, but his attention had been diverted.

Breathe, Jazz. Damnit!

I looked over at Lyric and found her eating while chatting it up with one of Melody's younger cousins. They were oblivious to the excitement amongst the adults. I was glad.

I refocused on what was going on in the room.

Melody came back to her seat as everyone else was returning to theirs. I sat quietly as the Thanksgiving festivities continued. I found myself peeking at him, covertly watching his every move.

"Baby, are you okay?"

I turned my attention to my girlfriend. "Yeah," I answered. "I'm just starting to feel a little funny in my stomach, that's all. I think I should probably go, though."

The disappointment showed clearly on her face.

"I'm sorry, baby," I told her. "I'll make it up to you. I just want to get home before it gets worse."

"I understand," she said sadly. "I won't be selfish, but will you at least meet my uncle? I am dying to introduce you two.

It felt like a cannonball dropped into my stomach, but I nodded.

After excusing myself from the table, I went and gave Mrs. King a kiss on her cheek and thanked her for having me and Lyric over for dinner.

"Why wouldn't I?" she said to me. "You're family now."

The sense of dread I felt as I followed Melody into the living room was so intense that it felt like a living, breathing monster.

"Uncle Arnie," she said, approaching the man who had

just sat down on the couch to eat his food.

He looked up and smiled at her. He looked at her as if she was his favorite person on earth.

I remembered when he used to look at me like that. It had put me at ease in my youth. He treated me like a sibling…until that night.

The night I learned he was nothing more than a predator.

"Hey, baby girl," he said, sitting his drink on the coffee table in front of him. "What's up?"

"I'm sorry to bother you," she began. "I know you're about to eat-"

"It's no bother," he interrupted. He glanced at me before turning his attention back to Melody. "What can I do for you?"

"I just wanted to introduce you to my girlfriend before she left," Melody explained. "She's not feeling too great, but I wanted the two of you to at least meet."

He turned his attention to me and held out his hand. It made my stomach churn to reach out and shake his outstretched hand.

He had that look again. I could sense the wheels turning in his head as he tried to place where he might have known me from.

"Uncle Arnie, this is Jasmine, but everyone calls her Jazz."

I watched his face as the light came on in his brain. The shock on his face was instant, but he concealed it just as quickly.

"Sorry, I can't stay longer," I blurted. "I'm not feeling too well."

"Well, I hope you feel better soon," he replied.

"Thank you," I said in return.

My mind had gone blank until Lyric walked up.

"I'm ready, Ma!"

He damn near snapped his neck to look at my daughter.

"And this lovely girl is Lyric, Jazz's daughter."

He quickly looked at the both of us before returning his attention to her. He reached out his hand again. "It's nice to meet you, Lyric."

Before she could shake his hand, I pulled her away.

"We really gotta get going," I said before maneuvering my daughter towards the front door.

Melody followed me and Lyric to my car.

"Are you sure you're going to be okay?" she asked. "I can come home, too, if you need me to."

"No, no," I told her, taking both of her hands in mine. "This is family time. Don't let me ruin it. Enjoy the rest of your Thanksgiving with your folks."

"Your hands are shaking," she noticed.

"That's because it's getting cool out here," I lied. "You should go inside. You don't have a jacket on. Go ahead. I'll text you and let you know that we made it home safely."

"You promise?" she asked. I could see the worry on her face.

"You have my word, baby."

She gave me a kiss on my lips. "If you say so," she said, then started walking towards the house, glancing back at me one more time before finally going inside.

I climbed in my car and started the engine. Before I could put my seatbelt on, the trembling that Melody felt in my hands moved up my arms, and before long, it had taken over my entire body.

"Ma, are you okay?"

I glanced over at Lyric as I tried to catch the breath that didn't want to cooperate with my body.

"I'm fine," I told her, gasping for air.

I rested my hands and my head on the steering wheel as I fought to regain my composure.

"No, you're not," my daughter contested. "I'm going to get Mel."

"I'm fine!" I told her, my hand snaking out and grabbing hers. "Just give me a minute!"

I forced deep breaths until I slowly started to calm down. I had to pull myself together before I scared the hell out of Lyric.

I looked over at her. "I'm okay," I told her. "And I didn't mean to snap at you. It was a little bit of anxiety, but I'm good now."

"It's okay," she responded with a tiny smile to reassure me. "Let's go home."

The ride home was a quiet one, but I was grateful for the silence. I was still slowly recovering from the panic attack I had in front of Melody's folk's house.

Once we were inside, I hugged Lyric and told her that I was going to lay down for a while. She gave me a "Yes, ma'am" and went into her bedroom.

I went into my room and laid in my bed. As I stared at the ceiling, I shook my head in amazement.

My demon, my rapist, and the father of my child was my girlfriend's fucking uncle.

I knew shit had been way too perfect.

THE RUNAWAY

I tossed and turned. Restful sleep had become a myth, and my dreams had become the nightmare I thought I'd forgotten about. I felt trapped. I was scared. I felt helpless. I felt hopeless.

"I ain't with this..."

My plea didn't matter.

"You got somethin' I want... I got somethin' you need..."

In my dream, I cried out the "no's" and "pleases" that I hadn't been able to voice in real life. But, my cries went ignored. He pushed into me, breaking past a lock that had never been touched, stealing the only bit of innocence a kid like me had. In my dream, there was no blacking out. I felt every thrust. I could smell the scent of blood in the air as he pounded away at my fragile insides.

I found myself stuck between my dream and reality. I could feel the tears on my face, but I couldn't open my eyes. I couldn't pull away from the images of someone who I once thought cared about me, destroying what was left of me.

The cool towel on my forehead pulled me free, and I sat straight up in my bed. For a moment, I had to focus and remember where I was.

"Jazz, it's okay."

Her voice was a salve that eased the pain in my soul.

She came to me, letting herself in with the key I had given her.

I looked at her.

"Whatever it is, it will be okay."

She moved closer to me and wrapped her arms around me. Finding solace in her embrace, I wrapped my arms around her and held on to her as she gently rocked me until I was able to fall asleep.

The next morning when I woke up, I was still fully dressed and so was she. I let her sleep and made my way to my bathroom to take a shower. I had hoped the shower would refresh me, but I was still drained from the night before.

After dressing, I went into the kitchen. Twenty minutes later, both Melody and Lyric were walking into the kitchen, following the smell of bacon and eggs.

"Good morning," I told them.

Lyric gave me a sleepy hug, and Melody gave me a kiss on the cheek.

"Both of you go wash your faces and hit those teeth, then come eat."

Breakfast was quiet but comfortable.

After clearing the dishes for me, Lyric said she was going to take a shower.

"Do you need me to do anything else before I go to the bathroom?" she asked.

I could still see the worry on her face. I felt horrible for giving her that scare the previous night. I had to figure out a way to make it up to her.

"No," I answered. "You're good to go, lil' mama."

I watched her go into the hallway to head to her bedroom before I turned around and faced Melody. I pulled her into my arms and gave her a kiss on the neck.

"Thank you," I told her.

"For what?" she wanted to know.

"Coming to me last night," I answered. "I needed that and I am grateful."

She held my face with both of her hands. "I love you, Jazz. I'm here for you."

I believed her.

"I love you, too," I told her, giving her a quick kiss on the lips.

"I'm going to run to my side of the fence to check out the house and get myself together," she informed me. "I'll be back."

"I'll be here," I responded.

I walked her to the door and gave her a kiss before watching her walk the distance between her house and mine. She waved before going inside.

I thought about the ring that I still hadn't presented to her and then wondered which house we would live in if she said yes. It's amazing how much a state of mind can change within minutes.

Melody hadn't been gone five minutes, when my doorbell rang. Thinking it was her and she'd left her key, I didn't even think to look through the peephole before I threw open the front door.

I should have.

There he stood as if he had stepped straight out of my nightmare from the night before.

What the fuck is he doing here? How the hell did he find me?

I said nothing as he stood before me.

"How are you doing?" he asked.

When I didn't respond, he continued. "Are you gonna

invite me in?"

I still stood dumbfounded, struggling to fight the anxiety rapidly building inside of me.

Get it together, I scolded myself. *Quit standing here like a fuckin' deaf mute.*

But, I didn't know what else to do.

Shake it off! You're not a kid anymore!

I blinked.

Face your demon!

Snapping out of it, I stepped aside. He took it as a welcome to come inside and crossed the threshold.

I took slow, deliberate breaths as he walked into my dining area. I followed him, not wanting him behind me. I glanced nervously towards the hallway, hoping Lyric wouldn't come out of the bathroom for at least another few minutes.

I watched him take a seat at my dining table.

I remained standing.

"How are you doing?" he repeated after making himself comfortable.

"Why are you here?" I demanded, refusing to lighten the pending conversation with unnecessary pleasantries.

"I want to get to know the person who has my niece's affections," he answered easily.

"Bullshit," I threw back. "Can we just cut the shit? I don't have time for this."

"You're still a little hardcore thing, huh?" he commented with a laugh that lacked mirth. "You were always a little firecracker. That's why I liked you so much. You didn't take no mess from anyone."

"I still don't," I retorted. "Now why are you here?"

"After you took my money and disappeared on me," he began, "I didn't think I'd ever see you again. Imagine how shocked I was to find you dating my niece."

"Yeah, okay. And?"

"So you can really understand how much of a bonus shock it was when I saw the girl."

I said nothing.

He continued. "Is she mine?"

"No."

My response was instant and resolute.

"So you've had sex with other guys?" he challenged. "Seeing you now, I can't imagine it."

"That's not your fuckin' business," I spat, feeling my temper rising.

He took a breath and had the audacity to sigh like I was testing him.

"Look," he began, "I'm not going to pretend like that night didn't happen. But, I'm not the same guy that I was back then. I'm trying to apologize-"

"What do you want?" I challenged. "A fuckin' cookie or a standing ovation or some shit? Do you think some apology is gonna fix everything?"

"I gave my life to Christ years ago-"

"Way to go," I interrupted. "If you go stand behind my car, I can get you a one-on-one with him real quick."

"I'm trying to make amends," he said.

His tone betrayed the fact that his patience was wearing thin. I didn't give a single fuck.

"Amends?" I asked in disbelief. "You want to make amends? You think you can make amends for taking my trust and throwing that shit away? You think you can make amends for stealing my virginity, the only thing that was mine, and replacing it with a baby and chlamydia? Really? Can you erase the night I tried to take my own life because of what you did to me? There is *nothing* you can do to make amends for any of it! Are you fuckin' kidding me?"

He stood up. "She's my daughter-"

"She is *not* your daughter!"

I stood toe to toe with him. My fear and anxiety were long gone. They had been replaced with animosity and the need to protect my child.

"You raped me!" I exclaimed. "You raped me and impregnated me, you fucker! And you gave me a gotdamn STD on top of that shit, with your dirty-dick ass! I wanted to end my fucking life because of you! I had to get a tat on my wrist to hide the fuckin' scars! And you think you can just come into my house giving me some bullshit talk about making amends? Fuck you! You don't get to claim her! She is *my* daughter, and I don't want you anywhere near her. As a matter of fact, stay the fuck away from me! I fuckin' hate you! Get the hell out of my house before I call the gotdamn cops or stand my fuckin' ground."

He opened his mouth to speak, but I cut him off.

"Get. The. Fuck. Out!"

Without another word, he turned to head to the front door, only to find Melody standing there. She looked like she had seen a ghost as she stared at her uncle.

"Is it true?" she asked in a low tone.

"Babygirl-"

"Uncle," she interrupted, holding her hand up to stop him. "Please tell me it's not true."

His silence was all the answer she needed.

"Oh my God, Uncle Arnie," she said, covering her mouth in horror.

Her anguish was immediate. Tears slipped from her eyes as she looked from him to me.

"Awww, babygirl," he began, "it was years ago. I'm not the same person."

"And that's supposed to make it better?" she asked, despair in her voice. After a moment, she spoke again. "You should go."

We both watched as he walked out of my front door.

She turned to me. "Jazz, baby, I'm so sorry. If I'd had any idea, I wouldn't have told him that you lived here."

Something in me snapped a little.

"*You* told him where I lived?" I asked, looking at her. "Why would you do that?"

"It just came up in general conversation last night," she answered. "He was asking about the love in my life-"

"And you just told him where the fuck I live?" I asked in disbelief. "He's a fuckin' rapist, and you just slid him my damn address."

"That's not fair, Jazz," she debated. "That's not-"

"Fair?" I yelled. "Who gives a fuck about fair?"

"Quit yelling at her!"

We both turned and found Lyric standing in the hallway.

"Stop yelling at her!" she repeated.

"You stay in a child's place," I told her. "Mind your business. Better yet, go to your room! Grown folks are talking."

"No-"

"Go to your gotdamn room!"

Her eyes widened, and she ran to her room and slammed her door.

"She didn't deserve that," Melody said quietly.

"Don't tell me what to do with my kid," I snapped. "As a matter of fact, you can get the fuck on, too!"

She couldn't have looked more shocked if I had hit her.

"What?" she said, dumbfounded.

"I said get the fuck on!"

She was quiet for a moment. Then, she took a deep breath.

"Okay." She walked to the door and opened it. "You'll regret this."

"Take me with you!" Lyric rushed out of her room and ran to Melody. "I don't want to be here anymore! Please take me with you!"

She cried and wrapped her arms around Melody. Seeing her do that cut me like a knife. So, I did the only thing I knew how to do. I lashed out.

"Oh, you wanna go with her? Go then! I ain't gonna stop you!"

"Jazz, you're taking this too damn far!" Melody scolded. "Stop it!"

"Stop what?" I yelled. "She'll be happier with you, so y'all go ahead. You heard her. She wants to be with you!"

Lyric was crying hard, and as much as I wanted to reach out to her, I didn't. I had gone too far, and I knew it. Not wanting her to reject me, I left her alone.

"This is stupid," Melody said, hugging my child to console her.

I turned away when I saw a fresh tear roll down Melody's cheek.

"You're dead wrong for this, Jazz."

She whispered words to Lyric in an attempt to ease her sorrow as they walked out the door. She didn't even bother to close the door, so I was forced to stand there and watch while my family walked away from me, leaving me to what I had once been accustomed to.

Emptiness and my solitude.

And it was my fault.

*   *   *   *   *

The quiet was killing me. They'd only been gone an hour, and I was ready to lose my mind. I had to get the hell away from there.

I went out to my backyard, pulled the cover off my Ducati 848, and stared at it for a minute. I remembered when I fell in love with the purple machine. I had to have it. I busted my ass, and it took me almost a year to raise the money. But, I did it and paid for it in cash. I hadn't ridden it since I moved into the house.

I needed the speed.

I needed to get away from there as fast as I could.

Ten minutes later, I was on the freeway weaving through the traffic, hitting ninety miles an hour and then ninety-five. I circled the city in almost no time. I did it twice before it hit me that I had nowhere to run to.

On a whim, I found myself pulling up to a house where I knew I had no business being. I climbed off my bike and made my way to the front door. Though I knew better, I reached up and pressed the doorbell anyway. To my surprise, she opened the door.

"Jazz, what are you doing here?"

"Hello, Jordan.".

RESPONSIBILITY

It had been a while since I'd been there. It had been a while since I'd felt this way.

I was high as fuck. For the first time in years, I got a hold of some weed. Rolling the blunt came back to me as if I had never stopped.

I hit it a few times, choking on the high-grade herbals before leaving my hotel room. The effects of it were still lingering as I laid on the oversized beach towel and looked out at the Atlantic Ocean.

After getting put out of Jordan's house, I didn't want to go home. I laughed at myself and shook my head as I recalled the events of the previous day.

I knew if she let me in, the rest would be easy.

And I was right.

I had her hemmed up in her bedroom in less than two minutes. We were both aggressive, both just wanting to get off. But, when it was time to seal the deal, I couldn't.

All I could think about was the woman who I'd just lost.

"Get out, Jazz. I'm sick of you playing with me. And this time, don't come back."

She had every right to be salty.

When I left her house, I promised myself that I would never go back. I knew better any damn way.

After only a few minutes of thought, I made the decision to go to Savannah. I got in touch with one of my clients, who also happened to be a weed man. I bought a bag, then went to the liquor store and got two bottles of gin before hitting the road. I was on the coast in less than three hours and lucked up on a room not too far from Tybee Island.

That night, I laid on the bed dying to call Melody and Lyric, but I was still being stubborn. More than anything, I felt like a fool.

I had faced Rich, now known as Arnez, and had slayed that demon. However, in doing so, I had created a new one in myself, taking my residual anger out on the people I loved. And now I was paying for it.

I laid there hitting my first blunt while taking shots of gin out of one of the plastic hotel cups. It had only been a day, and I missed my little family.

I cleared over half a bottle of gin before I threw up and passed out on the bed. My goal was to do it again the next day. I wanted to get fucked up until I couldn't feel anything.

Fate had other plans, I guess.

I was sitting at a local bar that evening opting to drink rum instead of the gin I had stored in my room. The room had gotten too quiet for me, and I felt the need to be around people. I was already feeling alright from the little bit of weed I had smoked before leaving my room. I just wanted to get a good buzz before going back to my room and finishing off the rest of the bottle that waited for me there.

"Jazz?"

I looked up and was surprised to see my realtor standing

there.

"Joi? How are you?"

"I'm great!" she answered. "Just waiting on Toya to come out the ladies' room. Date night."

"Oh okay," I replied. "What are you doing here?"

"We have a house here on the beach," she answered. "What about you? What brings you to Tybee? Vacation?"

I laughed, but there was no humor. "Something like that."

She looked at me for a second before speaking. "Something like that, huh? Need to talk?"

"Nah," I answered. "I'm good, but thanks."

Minutes later, I found myself sitting at a table with Joi and her wife, spilling my fucking guts to them. I was at least able to maintain and not cry like a little bitch in front of them.

"Go home, Jazz," Joi said after listening to my plight. "Well, after you sleep off this liquor and get a decent night's rest. *Then* go home to your family."

"But what if they don't want to deal with me anymore?" I asked. "My daughter already said she didn't want to be there with me."

"Well, can you blame her after the way you acted?" Toya chimed in. "I wouldn't want to be there, either."

"But," Joi added, "I'm willing to bet she didn't mean it. Everybody was running off emotion and negative energy. Go to them, apologize, take responsibility for what you did, and work your ass off to make it up to them. You owe them that whether they accept your apology or not."

"And put the bottle down," Toya added. "I went down that road before," she confided. "It almost destroyed me. Trust me when I say getting fucked up is *not* the solution."

So I listened to them.

The next morning, I left my liquor and the last little scrap of herb in the trash and hit the road, heading back towards Atlanta.

My nerves were shot as I pulled up to my house. I parked my bike in front of my car and looked over at the house next door. My heart raced as I walked over and climbed the steps. After taking a breath, I rang the doorbell.

Moments later, Melody opened the door. She didn't say a word. She just looked at me.

She wasn't going to be an easy win, if she could be won over at all.

I cleared my throat. "Can I speak to Lyric, please?"

"If she wants to speak to you." She walked away.

Moments later, Lyric came to the door. Her eyes were sad as she looked at me.

"Will you please come out here and sit with me so we can talk?"

She hesitated for a moment, and the lack of action killed me.

"Please," I added.

She unlocked the screen door and stepped out onto the porch. We walked over to the swing and sat down.

I inhaled. "I want to apologize for how I acted with you and Mel the other day," I began. "I was wrong, and I am so sorry. Neither of you deserved how I treated you. I didn't mean to hurt you or make you cry. I am so, so sorry, and I hope that one day you will forgive me."

She looked up at me with tears running down her face. "Do you love me?" she asked.

"Of course, I do," I answered emphatically. "Why would you think I don't?"

"Because you never tell me," she replied. "I've heard you

say it to Mel, but you've never said it to me. And then you said you wanted to die because you were pregnant with me."

"No," I debated. "That wasn't why I felt that way. I was still a kid, and I was scared, and I was hurt, and I was so damaged, and I didn't know any better. I was afraid you would end up like me. I didn't know anything about being loved, and I didn't want that for you. I would rather have died than to bring you into this world to live like I had. You've been the most wonderful thing to ever happen to me. And I do love you. I love you so much."

She fell into my arms and cried. I hugged her and felt tears on my own face.

"I love you," I repeated. "I'll try my damnedest to never hurt you like this again."

She sniffled. "You promise?"

"I promise," I told her. "Do you want to come back home with me?"

"Yes," she answered, wiping her tears away with the back of her hand. "But, I don't want to leave Mel. She's been sad, too. I heard her crying in her room. She always tells me she's okay, but I know she's sad, too. Are you going to apologize to her, too?"

"I plan to," I answered.

"I'm glad," she confessed. "I want you both to be happy again. I miss having two moms, and I love you both." She stood up from the swing. "I'll go get Mel so you can talk to her now."

"Thank you," I said, smiling at my daughter.

She gave me a big hug. "I love you, Ma."

"I love you, too," I told her. "And I promise to let you know every day for the rest of your life. Okay?"

"Deal!" she said before going inside the house.

A minute later, Melody came out onto the porch. She looked at me, arms crossed, waiting.

I got up and walked over to her.

"It's your turn," I began. "Baby, I am so-"

My apology was brought to a dead stop when her hand made contact with my face. For a second, I thought I saw stars.

"Don't call me baby," she hissed. "And you can keep your fuckin' apology!"

I didn't know what to expect, but it sure as fuck hadn't been *that.*

FORGIVENESS

My face still stung from the impact. "What the f-"

"Don't you dare come to me with some fuckin' apology, asking for forgiveness with a fuckin' hickey on your neck!"

I cringed on the inside. I had completely forgotten about it.

Fuck!

"You went to see her, didn't you?" she interrogated. "Is that where you've been all this time?"

"No-"

"I've been here miserable as hell, missing you like crazy, and all this time you've been off fucking your ex? I refuse to be your fool and let you run back and forth between me and her!"

"That's not how it happened-"

"Well, your neck says otherwise," she argued, digging into the mark with her fingertip. "If you have to debate on which one of us you want, *please* spare me and pick her. Please, please, *please* pick her."

I grabbed her by her arms and shook her. "Will you please shut the fuck up and listen?"

She looked at me, defiant but quiet.

"Yes, I went to her," I began. "And yes, I went to fuck. I could have. She was ready and willing. But, I didn't. I didn't have the heart to do it. It would've just been a fuck. I don't want that anymore. All I want is you."

She looked at me through damp eyelashes. "How can I believe you seeing this?" she asked. "How do I know I can trust you?"

"I guess you don't," I answered. "But, please give me the opportunity to prove myself to you. I love you. I'm still learning about this love stuff. I don't want anyone else to guide me but you and that little girl in there. I need you ladies. I need my family."

She was quiet. I could see her struggling with this.

"Look," I said, taking her hands. "Can we just start with you forgiving me? I'll be overjoyed if you give me that much. We can start from there."

She pulled one of her hands free from mine and touched the cheek she had just laid fire to.

"We can start from there," she said with a nod.

I pulled her close to me. "Thank you," I told her. "I love you."

"I love you, too, Jazz," she whispered. "Don't fuck this up."

"I won't. I promise."

For a minute, I just held her.

"Is it too soon to ask for a kiss?" I asked.

"A kiss?" she scoffed. "I outta bite that damn mark off your neck."

"Don't do it," I pleaded before she brought those soft lips to mine. "I've missed you, baby. I have issues and I'm hella scarred," I told her, then said, "Will you help me work through this?"

"I told you already," she replied. "I got you. As long as you act right, that won't change."

As I held her and she kissed me again, I knew there really was hope. It would take some time and I would have to show her that I was still worthy of her love, but I was confident that I would one day give her the velvet box that I had put in my dresser drawer.

"So does this mean we're a family again?"

We looked over and saw Lyric standing there.

"Yeah, I think so, kid," I replied.

It was the cheesiest moment I had ever experienced in my entire life, but I wouldn't have traded it for shit. I was happy. Like, truly happy. And for the first time in my entire life, I felt like I had a song worth singing.

"Love" itself was my new soundtrack.

ABOUT THE AUTHOR

Born in Little Rock, Arkansas, Olivia 'Renee' Wallace has loved writing since she was a child, penning her first reader's theater when she was in elementary school. As she grew more mature, so did her writing. In high school, she began writing teen-aged love stories featuring the teen heartthrobs of that era. By the time she was 25, she was writing short stories and sharing them online as a hobby. After completing her training with the Paul Mitchell Systems and becoming a hair care professional, Olivia accepted the fact that, though she enjoys doing hair, her true passion is and always has been writing. She is currently working on several projects to be released in the future. She believes that fiction can be romantic and steamy, yet also true-to-life.

This easy-going mother of three vivacious daughters considers herself a travel agent for mental getaways and she invites all who have an open mind to enjoy a vacation through her writing.

WORKS BY OLIVIA RENEE WALLACE

Novels:
She Say, She Say: A Modern Love Story
In Pursuit of Joi
Foolish Pursuits
Mimi's Heart

Short Stories:
A Blissful Glimpse
Crossed Boundaries

Anthologies:
Eros 369 (Contributor)
The Turnout Queens (Contributor)
Lustful Sins: A Sensual Compilation (Contributor)

Contact: www.Facebook.com/ReneeWallaceBooks

Made in the USA
Las Vegas, NV
28 January 2025

17142710R10115